MATTERS
OF HART

MATTERS OF HART

Marianne Ackerman

McArthur & Company
Toronto

First published in Canada in 2005 by
McArthur & Company
322 King St. West, Suite 402
Toronto, Ontario
M5V 1J2
www.mcarthur-co.com

This paperback edition published in 2006 by
McArthur & Company

Library and Archives Canada Cataloguing in Publication

Ackerman, Marianne
Matters of Hart / Marianne Ackerman.

ISBN 1-55278-600-5

I. Title.

PS8551.C33M38 2006   C813'.54   C2006-903376-5

Cover painting by Karen Thomson
Cover design by Tania Craan
Printed in Canada by Webcom

The publisher would like to acknowledge the financial support of the
Government of Canada through the Book Publishing Industry
Development Program (BPIDP) and the Canada Council for our publishing activities. The publisher further wishes to acknowledge the financial
support of the Ontario Arts Council for our publishing program.

10 9 8 7 6 5 4 3 2 1

To the memory of my mother,
Susan Kathleen Murphy

ও I ও

AMANDA

When I was five years old my brother Hart told me a story that cast a long shadow. He was thirteen, played a mean saxophone and excelled at hockey. He had bruises on both knees, and blue eyes that matched the ceiling of my room. What he said as we sat on the edge of the bed lodged in my mind like a feverish stranger and stayed there long after he'd countered with a denial. As time passed, I forgot about it. I imagine he did too, until one night last spring an unexpected knock at the door brought the whole thing roaring back.

The occasion was Hart's fiftieth birthday, a Saturday evening in May. His former wife, Sandrine, threw a surprise party at her home in Montreal. I flew up from New York and brought Mother out of her nursing home in a wheelchair. She'd suffered a stroke a few months earlier, which had weakened her limbs and clouded her mind. I had hoped the change of scenery would do her good, but it was obvious from the start that a noisy crowd wasn't the best place for an old woman who could barely remember her own children. Spring is a busy season at the publishing house where I work as an editor, so my thoughts must have been elsewhere.

The day of the party was an ordeal demanding patience and diplomacy from all of us who'd agreed to help. Sandrine had declared the guest list would consist of exactly fifty names – one for every year of Hart's life – friends, colleagues, acquaintances, an eclectic mix of people who'd either known him along the way or were significant in this vintage year. Sandrine is a philosophy professor at McGill University, which I mention by way of explanation, though perhaps it isn't one. She and Hart had been divorced for a decade but it was hard to see what had changed. They kept up a rhythm of fiery partings and bruised reconciliations, so that the state of divorce seemed less like an end of love than a mirror image of their marriage. At the time of Hart's birthday, they were on good terms.

Sandrine's field is the philosophy of mind. She'd launched her academic career in her twenties with a brilliant thesis on the theoretical potential for consciousness in inanimate objects. Her international reputation rests with the Institute for Advanced Creative Dynamics, which is situated at McGill and serves as the headquarters for everything she does. The 'Magic 50' guest list was deemed an aesthetically worthy idea deserving of mention in the IACD newsletter. It was not without certain practical problems.

Some guests who were invited solo would not commit to attending without their partners. A handful of people who weren't on the list heard about the party and were royally annoyed at being left out. Fifty on the nose proved a moving target. Faced with a last-minute cancellation, she was forced to haul in an eighty-year-old Greek bachelor who ran a dry cleaning business and occupied the basement apartment in her building. Zorba Parnopoulos was missing all but four teeth top and bottom so he rarely smiled broadly. When he did, his cheeks sank in like tiny black caves. It was his face Hart saw first when he walked through the door carrying a six-pack, ready to watch the hockey game Sandrine had video-taped for him the night before, as an excuse to get him over. When the birthday boy flipped on the light, we all jumped out from our hiding places, Mr. Parnopoulos leading the shouts. Hart dropped the beer and swore.

Sandrine owns a large Edwardian-era triplex on the Plateau Mont-Royal, a neighbourhood east of the mountain, which has become quite fashionable. She occupies the top floor, tastefully decorated in pale colours and clean lines that draw your attention to the ornate mouldings and orig-inal features. In the elegant double living room just inside the front door, she had set out an impressive buffet along with a generous supply of drink, served up by two impov-erished undergrads hired for the occasion.

Whatever the philosophical basis of Hart's fiftieth, I'm sure Sandrine secretly hoped for a moving tribute along the lines of *This Is Your Life*, where the guest of honour is reduced to tears by the appearance of long-lost loved ones. She'd spent years trying to melt down my brother. But the retrospective nature of the invitation list meant there were quite a few people who didn't know each other. The first hour was agonising. I did my best to chat-up wallflowers, introducing them to people with whom they might find something in common. Once a few drinks were poured, the mix of ages and backgrounds proved quite dynamic, though most people seemed far more interested in each other than in the birthday boy. Milling through the crowd, I began to wonder if the only traits Hart's so-called friends had in common were amnesia and a fierce need to score social points in the here and now. It seems the people you pick up along life's road don't always appreciate the lift.

Three men from his Racket Club stood in a corner all night and told private stories. Let out without their wives, his amateur-league hockey mates concentrated on serious drinking and making contact with a woman dressed in red. The prize for most sociable stranger went to Hart's old saxophone teacher, Mr. Munger, a legend from our childhood who came to the house and gave lessons in the front room. He had been an imposing figure in the sixties, and had stood up much better than my mother, who must have been about the same age. Virtually every woman present was prepared to give Leroy "Hotlips" Munger a lot of time, which may explain why Hart took up the instrument as an adolescent.

Despite Sandrine's hopes, those who stayed in the front rooms left early. The rest of us gravitated to the brightly-lit kitchen at the far end of a long hallway. By eleven it was packed. People were jammed against a sink full of ice and spilled out onto the balcony where they sat on recycling boxes, knocking hanging pots with wild hand gestures and bothering the neighbours with their laughter. Even Hart seemed to be having a good time. He'd managed to overcome his shock and proceeded to get cheerfully drunk. When he drinks, his blue eyes turn watery, his cheeks redden, and the prickly side of his personality gives way to a doll-like aura that some women find attractive.

Part of Sandrine's surprise was the presence of his latest girlfriend, Polly, who in the tradition of her predecessors was neither as physically striking nor as accomplished as

Sandrine. Polly was (and as far as I know, still is) in men's fashion. Hart was her current mission. For his birthday, she chose a spiffy new sports jacket, presented for the occasion. It covered up an insouciant slouch and hid the extra pounds he carried on a medium frame, making him appear almost dignified, even as he stood half-cut in the middle of his ex-wife's kitchen.

Sandrine is lean and fit, slightly taller than fair-haired Hart. She keeps her dark hair cropped short with an amazing precision that matches her mind. In the decisive moment, just as the night was about to leap from a blurry good time to a time that would change our lives forever, she put her hand on Hart's shoulder and leaned in, as if to speak only to him. I wish I had an actual photograph, though the image remains vivid. It was an annunciation scene, perfectly framed by the egg-yolk walls, aglow with the same tension we'd all felt hours earlier while standing in the front room, sucking in our breath, ready to shout, 'Surprise!'

Yet all she said was, "There's someone at the door to see you."

I was near enough to catch the taunt in her voice. Polly was standing beside Hart and reached for his hand. When we were paying fierce attention, Sandrine added, "It's a man. He says he's your brother."

Somehow, Mother had managed to lodge herself in the congested kitchen. She must have had help tilting the motorised wheelchair over a bulge of hardwood that rose like a speed bump in the hallway. As the only person sitting down, and claiming deafness, she forced people to lean over and raise their voices, which contributed to the boisterous pitch of conversation at the time of Sandrine's announcement.

Nevertheless, on the words *your brother*, the room fell quiet. I had my mother's profile in sight. Since the stroke, we could not be sure whether she understood or even listened to what was being said, but in this moment I knew she'd heard. The muscles in her neck tightened, her lips opened as if she were about to speak, though she'd said nothing for months. Instead, she closed her eyes and sighed.

Hart gave a short hiccup laugh.

Sandrine chirped, "I didn't know you had a brother."

Hart glanced at me and in a dry voice replied, "I don't."

Apart from traditional holidays and the odd lunch when business brought him to New York, I hadn't seen a great deal of Hart in recent years. I know nothing about high finance, and anyway, he rarely talked about his work, insisted it was temporary, that he would soon be getting into film, 'the art form of our time.' This I took as a thinly disguised criticism of fiction, which he once quipped was 'a crime against nature' – all those trees slaughtered in the cause of perishable prose. He was teasing me, of course, though his dark wit could sting. The night of the party, however, that side of him seemed far away. He was flattered by the attention, and it showed. In return, I was kindly disposed toward my big brother. I remember thinking that science must be right: being in the presence of common genes does induce a physiological state of well-being. I wished it were New Year's Eve, so he'd give me a big bear hug at midnight.

At least until Sandrine said, 'your brother.' I heard an echo: *our brother*.

Her words were a stone fired at my belly. As the back of his head disappeared through the doorway, I thought, no human being on the planet has made me suffer more than Hart.

The ceiling of my bedroom was covered with a popular wall-paper chosen by my mother before I was born, sky-blue background with huge cumulus clouds. I was sitting on the edge of the bed, wearing slippers. My feet didn't touch the floor. Hart reached over, took my hand and whispered, "Can you keep a secret?"

People rarely answer that question with a no; at the age of five, I wondered anxiously: will it be hard to keep?

The season must have been summer. He was dressed in shorts. One knee bore a thick, grubby bandage and the other a purple welt. Hockey injuries, as I recall, although why they would have lingered is a mystery, since the teams played on outdoor rinks that must have melted weeks before. My father often took me to games at Murray Hill Park on Saturday afternoon. I loved to sit on his lap and keep my eyes on Hart, who wore a fearsome mask and tended goal. Whenever the puck came his way, he dropped to his knees and I cried, "Ouch!"

While Hart expanded on the importance of keeping his secret, I focused my attention on his wounds, waiting to ask if he'd let me touch them. He must have noticed my mind wandering, because he squeezed my hand and said, "Okay, here it is."

I forced my eyes away from his knees.

"Remember when they brought you home from the hospital? Right after you were born?"

"Yes," I lied.

"Well, up until that time, there was someone else living in this room. He had to leave, to make space for you."

"Who was he?" I asked.

"Bill."

"Bill who?"

"Bill Granger, our older brother. See, there can only be two children in a house like this 'cause we've only got two kid bedrooms. So when Mum and Dad conceived you, they had to make a choice. I offered to leave, but they were *adamant*. They said I was too valuable to the team. That's why it had to be Bill."

"Where'd Bill go?"

"No idea. They wouldn't say."

I wanted to ask what he meant by 'conceived me.' Why were they 'adamant?' Even at thirteen, my brother had an impressive vocabulary. He hardly ever came to the dinner table without a new word. Mother was convinced Hart would some day become a famous writer. Dad, who was a doctor, favoured science. He said he wished he'd taken that path himself instead of devoting his life to the practical cause of illness. Hart was Daddy's great hope.

A precocious child, Hart had taught himself to read at three and excelled at everything he touched. He was sociable and smart and funny too. But as soon as school tests identified an IQ near genius, our ever-cautious parents panicked. Fearing he'd be spoiled, they stopped drawing attention to his wit or rewarding him in any way for showing off. Looking back on it now, I wonder if their decision to ignore his gifts might not have had something to do with what happened, or least offer a clue as to why Hart never followed up on his many talents.

Despite my parents' reluctance to praise, I sensed the glow when he dropped a new word into the dinner table conversation or quoted some wise remark from his reading. In my five-year-old eyes, my big brother was a god, so tall and handsome, and unfathomably smart.

As he whispered the tragic story of Bill, my head spun but I couldn't seem to formulate a question. Hart's physical presence, his grip on my hand, made it difficult to concentrate. He sealed my curiosity with a warning: "Don't ever, ever bring this up to Mum and Dad. They feel bad enough as it is. If you say anything to Mum, she'll be utterly devastated. Do you understand?"

I said I did.

"Course, they love you a lot," he continued. "So do I. Still, it's a shame we had to sacrifice Bill."

I looked around the room, at the dolls and teddy bears, the white table and chair set and rocking horse and suddenly all my precious things seemed to float, as if they'd just come unstuck from the surface and were about to go back inside me. As the child of progressive parents and the daughter of a doctor, I'd seen pictures of my mother's womb with me curled up in a ball. I assumed I belonged to her body, and by extension, that all my things belonged to me, and the world worked that way: you come out of someone who loves you and whatever you love comes out of you. Now there was Bill, an older boy who had packed up his things and slipped out of a house of love and gone somewhere. I was mesmerised by the thought of a strange deity inhabiting my room, one who had been banished a few seconds before my arrival. I was sure I could smell the lingering odour of his gym socks.

"Was he bigger than you?" I asked.

"He was."

The secret was terrible, and real. It explained why my parents were proud of Hart and treated me like a poor, fragile mistake. A flawed child, who had to be taken back to the hospital for repairs. I was sure they loved me, but it was love soaked in fear. Now I understood. My existence had come at a terrible price and we weren't finished paying yet. It all made sense: my many trips to the doctor, tests, operations. The way my mother hugged me, assured me I was beautiful, thereby planting doubt.

I did not question Hart's revelation. But I no longer believed his wounds. Looking down at his bandaged knee, I decided it was plump and phoney. While I tried to think of a question worthy of his wisdom, his eyes brimmed with anticipation, his ever-agile mind preparing an answer that would prove the existence and (thanks to me) the loss of Bill. So I whacked his bandaged knee. He howled, and punched me hard. I ran off wailing to Mother who demanded Hart come downstairs, but he'd already gone into his room and locked the door.

Wrapped in her arms, I cried myself weak over the loss of poor Bill, banished from our family so that I could have his place. Yet it would be false to say I felt guilty. I was suddenly relieved, ecstatic. Following the secret to its logical, selfish conclusion, I knew I had escaped a terrible fate, a lifetime spent scrunched up inside my mother's stomach beside mashed potatoes and coffee. Thanks to Bill, I had a room, pink slippers, dolls and teddies.

That night I climbed into bed and lay awake for what seemed like a very long time. After dark, the ceiling clouds disappeared and were replaced by a milky way of fluorescent stars. Looking up at the night sky, I cast my racing mind back to the day he left, then forward, to the cold, misty field of emptiness where he must be now. Thus I began to share my room with the memory of my brother Bill.

Had he stopped there, Hart's breathless fabrication might have faded like any other childhood nightmare. Instead, he kept up a stream of carefully prepared references calculated to maintain my interest. He pointed out Bill's one-of-a-kind tumbler with a moose head decal. He showed me which man he'd used for monopoly. Then he found a baseball glove Bill had left behind by mistake, and claimed it had to be thrown out. I begged him to let me keep it but he said if Mum saw the glove, she'd be reduced to hysterical tears, go insane and ruin the family. So I waited till he left the house, slipped into his room, took it out of a dresser drawer and hid it under my mattress. The smell of leather seemed to permeate the sheets. I was terrified of discovery.

The following September, I started school at Roslyn, and was relieved to find I'd been assigned my own hook in the cloakroom with a cubby above it for my lunch. I smuggled the glove in my koala bear backpack, and kept it hidden all winter, wrapped up in a sweater. The glove seemed to reek of leather and sweat. Walking home each afternoon, I wore my coat unbuttoned even in winter and took in great gulps of air so that no trace of Bill would linger when I walked in the door. In June we had to take everything home. I wanted desperately to hang onto my memento, but fear of damage to our family kept me strong. I gave the glove to Kenny Wilkinson, a boy in my class.

Then there were the pictures. Mum, Dad, Hart aged six, with a huge rip down the side of the photograph where

Bill's image had been removed. No trace of the missing son could remain inside the walls of our home. When I obediently got down on my knees to beg, he handed over one mutilated snapshot, but warned me that should it be discovered, he'd deny everything. I kept the picture locked in my diary and was careful to write nothing about Bill, a difficult omission that deepened my sense of betrayal and smothered the joy of writing for a very long time.

In 1967, my father was promoted to chief surgeon at the Montreal General Hospital and we moved into a bigger house on Grosvenor Street. By then I was old enough to follow the logic: surely our parents could have moved to a bigger house before I was born, with enough rooms for three children. I'd noticed several of my schoolmates slept two to a room. Why didn't my two brothers get bunk beds? Just as I was about to confront Hart with the irrefutable proof that he had lied, he confessed.

How he confessed! He didn't just say, "I lied. There is no Bill." He came into my room in the middle of the night, woke me up with a flashlight pointed at my eyes. Tears running down his cheeks, lips swollen as though he'd been sucking on some poisonous weed, he stroked my hair and begged for forgiveness. Once again I had to swear never to tell anyone, most of all Mum and Dad.

"I did a terrible thing," he murmured over and over. "I should never, ever have told you that story. Do not believe me. I'm evil. I will go to hell. Keep your distance from me, Amanda. You're a good girl. Save yourself. I am the devil."

That was the essence of Hart's confession, though it seemed to go on all night. When he finally finished bludgeoning me with self-accusations and semi-comprehensible ravings, I was exhausted and unable to sleep. He seemed to feel much better. He thanked me for understanding and kissed me. His spit tasted like milkweed juice and made me shiver.

When he'd gone, I put on the light. I had no idea why Hart had been so churned up by what he wanted to say (to this day, I'm still not sure). But I was no longer afraid. My mind was clear and seething. Carefully, word-by-word, I replayed everything he'd said, struggling to sort out the implications. Despite his hand wringing and hysterical sobs, he definitely had not denied the existence of Bill. He simply regretted telling me.

By morning, I'd convinced myself that the truth about our long lost brother was far darker and more complex than Hart had been able to convey. He might be a boy genius with a brilliant future in any number of fields, a cast of spectacular friends, musical talent and athletic prowess to burn, while I struggled with my small body, a hole in my heart that required operations, and one passion: reading books. But from that night on, I knew Hart also had his limitations. There were issues surrounding the history and health of our family that he was incapable of understanding, though maybe he had coped as well as he could. It hit me then that there were things I knew that Hart did not. He possessed facts but I felt the truth in my bones, and my feelings were somehow more important than Hart's facts. Stronger, more durable.

With the cold shock of Hart's confession, I discovered in myself a source of protective, big sister love for the ace goalie. I no longer worshipped him, I was concerned about him, and concern gave me confidence. That winter, when I saw him drop to his knees on the ice, watched the puck go whirling through his legs and score a point for the enemy

team, I knew there were tears behind the mask. I no longer
said, "Ouch!" I shook my fists and yelled, "Get up!"

Sandrine's approach to other people's lives frequently includes
full-blown scripts and dramatic scenes. One of her fantasies
for Hart's fiftieth was that he would pick up his sax again
and blow the roof off. While they were married and trying
to live at the same address, his so-called wild side drove her
crazy. But she seemed to relish symptoms of creativity in an
ex-husband.

At the beginning of the party, Hart had spied the instrument case lying on the brocade ottoman, and snarled. Despite
murmurs of gratitude and considerable liquor, he was not
totally reconciled to having his Golden Age revealed to people he rarely if ever bothered to look up. A command performance was, he proclaimed, an invitation to humiliation.
Hart was not about to play the saxophone. But Leroy Munger
did.

While Hart went to the door to greet the mystery guest,
Leroy played like a wounded demon. Long, sad notes strung
together with excruciating clarity. A sublime blues solo, it
seemed to come from far away and settle on us all like a
melancholy cloud. I wish I could identify the tune, offer an
obscure and weirdly appropriate title that would make true
blues fans nod sagely and say, *how apropos*. I can hum the
melody and pick it out on the piano, but even the most
fanatical scholars have been unable to provide me with a clue.
Nor could Munger recall what he played that night, so words
will have to do: It was a song that filled you with sorrow yet
somehow made you grateful. An aching wave of knowing,

it drowned out old life and opened up a way to the new, made you ready, eager. And the only thing do was close your eyes, pick up a suitcase. Twenty seconds, maybe thirty, that song was an invitation to fly.

I watched my mother listen, saw her lean towards the song, drink it in with open lips. The conversation didn't actually stop; people went on talking but their bodies swayed. I had a strange desire to laugh and cry, and made no effort to resist.

Then we heard the shouts.

Hart's friends from the hockey team had pretty well accomplished their mission to become obscenely drunk. A witness claimed the trouble started when they became involved. As far as I was later able to reconstruct the scene, Hart and the new arrival had exchanged words at the door, which two burly defensemen interpreted as trouble. They stepped in, which explains the shouts. But we never did discover a wound to account for the amount of blood that covered the stranger's face and shirt when he was led through the kitchen to a bathroom at the far end. Maybe it was just a nosebleed, a nervous reaction. I didn't ask.

Still, the blood did not obscure his main features. He was a good six feet tall, muscular, with a full head of dark hair and a ruddy complexion. He was steeped in one of those imitation-leather colognes that lingered as he passed. He stayed out of sight a long time. When he came out, he was wearing one of Hart's old t-shirts, which Sandrine just happened to have on hand. The strong scent was gone. He looked dazed. I noticed his skin wasn't naturally ruddy. As he stared at the back of my mother's head, he was blushing, as though the blood rushed through his body at a fierce rate.

Hart's obnoxious teammates disappeared into the night with a blast of hale and raunchy farewells. Somebody put on a CD. The new guest, the man who blushed in my mother's presence, accepted a cold beer and apologised for the mess. He leaned down close to my ear and said, "You must be Amanda."

I nodded.

"I'm Neil Springer. Sorry. I had no idea there'd be a party. I'm up here from Vermont for a Rotary Club convention. Went by the nursing home. They gave me this address. Don't know what got into me. I should have phoned first . . . or waited." His brown eyes jumped around the room, landing on my mother, who was slumped down in her wheelchair, apparently oblivious to her surroundings.

I said, "You're my brother, aren't you?"

He lowered his voice, so nobody heard but me. "Well, your half-brother."

Then he chug-a-lugged his beer and set the bottle down. "I'm up at the Holiday Inn. The boys are waiting. I'd better go."

On his way out, he stopped, turned around and looked at me. He just stood there, smiling, and it felt as good as a bear hug on New Year's Eve. Then he nodded and disappeared.

I got myself a Scotch and went out to ask Hotlips Munger for a dance. That tune I can remember: "Heartbreak Hotel." Not exactly original, but it fit my crazy, wild state to perfection. I don't remember feeling that kind of thrill, well, since Kenny Wilkinson.

After giving the baseball glove to Kenny, I had to put up with months of teasing from the other kids, who swore I had a crush on him. Eventually, I stopped minding. We stayed friends through high school, and though he never asked me out, I could tell he was proud of the compliment. When we graduated, he even offered to give me back the glove, but by then I'd dismissed Hart's tall tale. At least, I was too stubborn to admit the memento meant anything, so I declined. I think I said, "Keep it," and took a deep breath, a gesture I was working on at the time. It makes your breasts heave slightly and imprints whatever you've just said on a guy's mind. Who was I kidding? I desperately hoped Kenny would never, ever part with that glove, and I would always know where to find it. The glove was part of a terrible secret, blurred by time into a vague memory of loss. Kenny bore the burden like a gallant knight.

Next to getting boys to ask me out, my chief interest in high school was literature. I read every novel I could find, and rated them according to my own system. What counted was the initial flash, the moment when your interest clicks and you just have to know how things are going to turn out. As long as you keep wondering, you keep on reading.

At university I discovered literary theory, which temporarily dented my enjoyment of stories but fortunately did not completely kill it off. After graduation I burned my theory notes and returned to first principles: to trust in the promise a writer makes, to hunger for the power of revelation and the desire for surprise. The exhilaration of being turned inside out by what happens next. I got a job at a publishing house, and after a few unpleasant scuffles, found a manuscript that answered all my cravings. We published it. Many, many readers agreed with me, so I was on my way.

As a literary editor, I've come to know a variety of creative individuals. Early on, I began to recognise their inventions for what they are: not exactly lies, rather, pools of energy, sparks that must be passed on. The more the spark burns, the more books sell. If there's a secret to my success as an editor, it lies with my insatiable need to know how a story ends. I can see in the raw chaos of a fresh manuscript the details that should be cut, and those that must stand in order to pull the reader on.

From my years in academe, I retained a belief in the importance of text over author, a choice not always shared by the marketing department, where personality is king. Most writers, I've noticed, want two things (in addition to becoming rich and famous): they want to be loved and they want their butts kicked. In other words, they're looking for mothers and fathers. I enjoy the thrill of moving down a page of words and finding the spark, following stories that go off on side roads and then veer back and hit you in the face. Happy or sad, it doesn't matter. Stories end.

Unlike literature, where structure provides at least an aesthetic equivalent to resolution, the story of "Bill" did not end cleanly or dissolve into a higher purpose. It sputtered and settled into a slow burn. My half-brother, Neil, is a welder who lives in Sherbourne, Vermont. He is married to Wanda, who works part-time at a chain store. They have three children, fourteen, seventeen and nineteen. Their youngest boy, Jack, is close in age to my older son, Jacob.

Since the night of Neil's first appearance, my mother has suffered another stroke, so she cannot effectively be quizzed about this secret from her past. Neil's research – which led him to our mother and the party – uncovered all we will ever know. He was born when she was seventeen, at a home in Vermont for unmarried, pregnant girls. After giving him up for adoption, she returned to Montreal, trained as a nurse and got a job at the Montreal General, where she met my father. As far as we could see, they lived happily ever after. Did my father, long since gone, know about the baby? Was Hart's invention of "Bill" pure co-incidence, or had our mother given hints? We'll probably never know.

Anyway, Neil is a big-hearted man, a well-adjusted human being with an intense love of family life and wonderful children. Wanda has come more slowly to the idea of a new family, but their kids are ecstatic. I cannot say I ever imagined having someone like Neil as a member of my family – we have little in common but our mother – and yet there are times when I think I've always known him; that the past was a kind of limbo, an unfinished story. Somehow his absence drove everything – my work, my quest to know and embrace America, to succeed in New York. I am prepared to say I sensed the existence of Neil in the phantom Bill.

The only person who wasn't thrilled about the discovery of our missing brother was Hart. The morning after the birthday party, Neil and I met for lunch. We basically got acquainted and agreed that he and Wanda should come to New York, where they could meet my husband Tom, and our children, Jacob and Mark. That first visit went very well. They saw a Broadway show and enjoyed getting to know the big city. After that, we planned a trip to Montreal so that Neil could call on Mother and then the whole family would go out to dinner.

It was a disaster! Hart moved from quiet hostility to scorn and finally left the restaurant in a huff without touching the bill, which is unusual. Being generous and well-off, he normally insists on treating everyone in sight. The following day I dropped by his office. I was furious about his rudeness and wanted to tell him so. He made a few sarcastic swipes at Neil that in retrospect sounded suspiciously like jealousy. Since then we haven't had much contact.

I love Hart dearly and always will. But I have a feeling this rift may grow worse with time. I am struggling to understand him. Maybe he has carried a burden of guilt over the way he tortured me with the story of Bill. (His strange, middle-of-the-night attempt at repentance only made it worse.) Now this burden has been shifted onto our lost brother. Subconsciously, Hart may have cast Neil as his surrogate self, and is forcing him to bear the loathing, the guilt, the bile Hart kept caged inside for years. This would explain why a childless fifty-year-old, who is weighted down with misspent intellect, cannot accept a half brother with great kids, and is willing to sacrifice his only sister, because she *can* accept Neil. Hart feels bad because he lied to me! This, in my opinion, is the deepest truth. His excuse, if he has one. I cannot imagine another.

There are smaller points that may illuminate his animosity: Hart is losing his hair, at least it's thin and turning grey. Neil, though several years older, has a full head and could pass for being in his early forties. Hart has spent more money paying for his mistakes than Neil will ever earn, but Neil has a satisfying trade and a loving wife who thinks he's a stellar success. He is deeply involved in philanthropic causes: Kiwanis, Rotary Club, junior coaching, and his Church.

Another fact slipped out during the course of our fateful family dinner in Montreal, a detail that may have also had a part to play. Actually, Wanda told us about it. Around the time Hart made his spooky confession and drove the entire Bill story deeper into my pre-pubescent subconscious, Neil was drafted from his college hockey team and signed up with the Boston Bruins. He played one season as forward and scored a couple of goals before suffering a knee injury that took him off the ice forever. He walks with a bit of a limp. He's still got the photos and his Bruins hockey sweater.

According to Neil, a half-season in the NHL hardly constitutes a brilliant athletic career, but I think he's far too modest. When Wanda mentioned he played Number 10 for Boston, I shrieked, "Amazing!" then clamped my hands over my mouth and laughed till tears rolled down my cheeks. I was just so incredibly proud of him, yet somehow, not at all surprised. Neil/Bill as a professional hockey player seemed totally plausible. Inevitable. Of course, the life this mysterious brother lived outside our house would have been rich and meaningful; and there he was in person, a warm, cheerful, normal human being prepared to love us all.

Under other circumstances, Hart might have taken this information in stride. But immediately after the exchange about hockey, he left the restaurant. For weeks afterwards, he wouldn't return my calls and when I finally caught him in, he had nothing to say.

A few weeks later, Sandrine phoned to tell me he'd left Montreal, and gone off to L.A. to write a screenplay. He'd been threatening to do this for years, but I never thought he actually would. Sandrine had only a vague idea of what had happened that night. She didn't seem to take much interest when I tried to explain. In fact, thinking about it now, I realise she didn't seem at all disappointed to have her ex-husband living south of the border, out of earshot.

I guess I should be grateful for the shadow Hart cast on my childhood. Although it was not his intention, his fabrication set me on a path, opened me to the thrill of an unpredictable, unfathomable, unfinished story. Hart gave me my life's work.

I haven't given up on my middle brother. I remain open. As I've said, I love him. But there comes a point when a man's demons are his own business. So instead of worrying where he is or why he hasn't called, I am content to wait for news. I like to imagine he is thirteen again and living much the way Bill lived those early, formative years, estranged from his true family. He's out there somewhere in a misty field, eyeballing the emptiness.

❧ II ❧
LENA

Lena Aurbach was naturally slight with fine features and thin blond hair that hung like parted drapes. She was sensitive to the sun and applied layers of sunscreen to keep it away. She even rubbed her dog Gustav's nose, although after a week on the Pacific coast he still thought of the cream as food and licked it off when her back was turned.

Berliners by birth, they were mid-way through an ambitious circle-tour of the United States when Hart found them sitting on a bench by the ocean, gazing at the sunset. He couldn't say what caught his eye first, Lena's delicate beauty or Gustav's hold, the way he thumped his feathery tail impatiently, as if it was he who held her on a leash and not the other way around.

The sight of Lena's white cane leaning against her backpack drew him to a stop. A talisman of vulnerability, it made him want to say point-blank: go home, Venice Beach is no place for a blind girl. Instead he opened the conversation with a gentle word to Gustav, and thirty minutes later she was sitting on his back porch sipping Campari while he fired up the barbecue.

Of all the places they'd visited so far, California most closely resembled the America inside Lena's head. It smells white, she said, like an overexposed photograph, sea salt and fast cars, a wonderful, hectic dream.

Hart intended to warn her against talking to strangers. She must have seen it coming. "I don't usually go off with people I don't know," she assured him. "But Gustav likes you. Anyway, this is a special day, nothing bad can happen."

The day was September 10, 2001, her birthday. Almost twelve years since the Berlin Wall had come down, and twenty-four since she'd been born. She had lived half her life on the other side of a great divide, both symbolic and concrete. A dramatic soul prone to superstition, Lena was on the lookout for meaning in odd places. She was determined this day would be memorable. She had built their trip around it. She kept the illusion of blindness simple. The white cane was a prop, Gustav, a perfect straight man.

Her acting teacher claimed the key was to refine peripheral vision. Never look a person in the eye. Maintain a vacant stare and watch the edges. She had taken theatre classes to relieve the boredom of training as a nurse (her parents' idea). Lacking natural sympathy for those weakened by illness, she preferred to meet people on their feet. The act of blindness was a game that let her see what is normally kept hidden.

As Hart tossed plates and cutlery on the table, and uncorked a bottle of Napa Valley sauvignon, Gustav followed every move. Lena watched too, when Hart's back was turned. He reminded her of her father. The beginning of a belly rolled out over his blue jeans but he had solid shoulders and thick arms. She saw him start to light a candle, then think better of it. Instead, he left the porch light on. It lit them up like a stage.

For moments like this, she kept her lips pursed in a faint smile so if the urge to laugh took over, it wouldn't seem unusual.

Hart's questions were tactful. He didn't come right out and say, how does a blind girl find her way around a foreign country? Or, when did you go blind? His admiration was obvious.

She told him she had friends and contacts in every city they were visiting, people who could show her around, and Gustav was a brilliant guide. He would remember the way back to the youth hostel, only a few blocks away. He was capable of inflicting serious bodily harm should trouble arise.

Lena was wearing a short skirt. Bare legs crossed, she dangled a sandal loosely on the toes of one foot. Hart took long appreciative looks at her legs but there wasn't a hint of flirtation in his voice.

"Would you like me to cut it for you?" he said, setting a plate in front of her. "I mean your steak?"

"Please."

He'd grilled one for Gustav too, who growled as Hart approached Lena's side to cut their meat into bite-sized pieces. She reached down and petted the dog's mane, then felt for a fork and began the delicate act of eating blind.

From across the leafy patio garden, a woman stood behind a lace curtain, observing the candleless dinner. A Quebec-born actress, she had starred in a few blockbusters directed by a famous American, who became her husband for a while. When Hart moved into the house next door, he recognised her immediately, though she'd pretty well given up acting and was writing her memoirs. She had noticed him sitting on the back deck, nodding off in front of his laptop, and struck up a conversation.

She was glad he wasn't aloof like the fresh young thing who owned the house, a character actress who pined for stardom but spent most of her time running after Off-Off-Broadway plays. He was mature, and like herself, facing the challenge of a blank screen, a solitary ordeal full of hope and despair. He was willing to swap platitudes over a board fence covered with clematis. Once, they got drunk together, but it blew over in the daylight. From then on, they had an unspoken agreement not to start anything that would require discussion.

Lena nibbled at her salad while Hart studied her movements. The actress watched them through binoculars. Among the vanities that plagued her was a reluctance to admit needing strong glasses. Her doctor suggested laser correction, but she refused. She kept the computer screen on 16-point font and learned to choose fruit by touch and smell. Often she faked, falling back on the skills of her profession.

As Hart played the attentive host, she decided he would end up bedding this lovely young woman, and the idea cheered her. She imagined them stretched out on silk sheets, bathed in soft light, just like a movie. He was lonely. He pretended to write but was blocked by some unexplained woe. He often played blasts of music at noon, mood-lifting tunes that made the windows shake.

She turned away, switched on the television, leaving the sound low. Their voices drifted in through the open window.

It was dark by the time Hart and Lena finished eating. He had killed the bottle of wine and under the porch light's glare, his head ached. Thinking he would not easily forget the dazzle of Lena even under starlight, he flipped off the switch. She seemed to relax in the darkness. Head resting on her hands, she asked him about Montreal, a city she hoped to visit some day.

"People claim it's European," she said, "which is what they say about New Orleans, but they're wrong. It's all totally, unmistakably American."

Emboldened by wine, Hart ventured a sensitive question, "How can you experience these places and speak so confidently when . . ."

"Places have their own unique sounds and smells," she said. "Like original music, or perfume."

Hart closed his eyes to test her theory, but his senses were untrained. All he saw was Lena's lithe silhouette, glowing in the dark.

"And I'm not totally blind," she added, using the word for the first time. "I can see vague shapes. I can't read signs or recognise people, but light and dark, yes, I see the difference."

As they talked, an idea for a movie began to build in his mind, the story of a dog and blind girl making their way across America. A tragedy, of course; all this beauty and vulnerability could only meet a violent end. The thought sickened him but the idea was compelling, a feminist, youth-oriented road movie exploring the cruelty and kindness of America. From then on his questions concerned things a writer would need to know. Some of Lena's answers sounded silly, a few downright unlikely, but he pressed on, careful not to jeopardise access to this living source of inspiration, the one ingredient that had been absent from his oasis of solitude.

He had come to L.A. to write *Exoneration* (working title), a forensic thriller based on a treatment written years earlier during a single clairvoyant night, a creative binge following the worst week of his divorce from Sandrine. All he needed was time.

Since turning fifty, he'd made a few bold decisions concerning people and work. This was one of them. On the human front, he resolved to distance himself from certain individuals whose affection had begun to weigh, including his sister Amanda and their mother. He handed his files at Harvin Investments over to his partner, Vince Bailey, who'd been burning to run things his way for ages. He made no great pronouncements or predictions. He did not sit down to write a screenplay with visions of glory dancing in his head. Nor did he think himself a genius, or even that genius was required. He figured that by a certain age most intelligent, creative individuals had one producible full-length feature film in them; a serious commitment would shake it out. All he had to do was make time for typing.

The chance to sublet a furnished house in the epicentre of movie land fell into his lap the day after he resolved to leave Montreal. An actor he met at a party knew someone who had a place in Venice, California, a few blocks from the ocean. It was quiet and blissfully sparse. He found the days long and a little too hot for work. A month went by and still he hadn't even gotten around to reading the treatment. Instead, he'd skimmed a few how-to books and racked up a huge bill on the movie channel. He was bored and faintly depressed by the dearth of actual typing. Until Lena poked her ruby toenails into view, the realisation that he would never write *Exoneration* had stayed on the level of unconscious malaise.

As they talked, he had a powerful feeling she had come into his life for a purpose. Through her, the future would present itself. He was grateful, and resolved to give her a slice of the spoils.

At ten o'clock the actress went to bed but as soon as she closed her eyes, fatigue disappeared. She pondered her fellow Quebecer's dedication to the art of conversation, and his other, more delicious modes of communication. She hadn't noticed Lena's white cane. She figured she knew young women well enough to know that you don't spend an evening with a charbroiled slab of prime rib unless the man's demeanour is tempting. The girl's reticence led her to doubt her own judgement, to wonder whether Hart was an attractive man. By industry standards, no, he wasn't star material. But he could hold his end of a conversation and he seemed to take a genuine interest in women.

Throwing back the covers, she picked up the binoculars for another look. The porch light was out, still their voices bubbled through the night. Reaching for the bedside phone, she dialled his number, let it ring three times, and hung up. This should bring chatter to a close, she thought, smiling, and climbed back into bed.

When Hart went inside to answer the phone, Lena took advantage of his absence to stand up and smooth the wrinkles from her skirt. The bites of steak she'd eaten felt heavy in her belly. She shovelled the rest to Gustav, who ate like a wolf and began tugging on his leash. The day would soon be over. An important day, yet it had left no significant traces. She thought of her parents. Doting professionals, determined to have their precious only child find a place in the fast-moving world of unified Germany, they hadn't understood her decision to travel. Their graduation present was a substantial sum of money, which they expected she'd use to buy an apartment of her own. Blowing it all on a trip around America was not their idea of a good investment. And travelling alone? Not alone, she had protested, Gustav is a clever beast, impossible to dupe.

Without the mask of blindness, Lena was shy, which, coupled with youth and beauty, meant she was more often stared at than drawn into conversation. For long stretches of the journey she had been lonely and bored. Time stretched out like an endless sidewalk between a few memorable encounters; hours had to be filled. Two or three bad days running and she'd begun to think what all young spirits do in times of great disappointment, that maybe her parents were right. Homesickness settled in like a sudden change in weather. Meeting Hart had been a welcome respite. She was glad of conversation, but by the time of the phone call, she was aware conversation was running out.

"Be patient," she whispered to Gustav. "When the stranger returns, we'll say goodnight and go."

By the time Hart picked up the receiver, the phone had stopped ringing. He listened to the dial tone for a few moments, then checked the message screen. Unknown Caller. That's what it said when someone phoned from Montreal. He dialled Sandrine. The moment he heard her say hello he knew she hadn't called him. This was not the voice of a woman sitting by the phone. It was a half-sleepy almost sexy hello. Meaning she was not alone.

Most of the time, Hart wanted nothing more than to hear his ex-wife had moved on and found a new man, someone ready to soak up all that latent domestic energy, to grab hold of her objections and do the deed itself, reproduce, plunge into family life and leave solitary types like him to fend for themselves on Friday night. He was weary of feeling responsible for Sandrine. Worse, he was fed up with his own addiction to their dance.

Still, when he heard her sultry hello and imagined her lying naked beside a stranger, he did not immediately rejoice. He knew the music and perfume of that room the way Lena knew New Orleans, as a pure, visceral flood of sensation requiring no pictures. He was in Sandrine's bedroom, or the room was in him. Skylight illuminating a wall of exposed brick, hardwood floors, an iron bed, antique bathtub with claw feet scarcely hidden behind a screen of glass brick, it was a room designed for leisurely love and Sunday morning breakfast, because Sandrine was the kind of woman whose designs included a man. He had been there, soaked up the warmth, felt the weight of expectation. It irked him that someone else was there now. Jealousy wears many masks, and one of them is love. Held dangling by her breath, he knew he had come to L.A. to get away from Sandrine. He should say it, now. Tell her his call had been a mistake, like every other call. This must be the last call.

Instead, all he said was, "Sandrine!" It came out all wrong, hoarse and pleading. She did not reply and in the emptiness, a jab of pain started at his shoulder and shot straight down, taking his breath away.

He wanted to say *help* but the pain cut right to left, a lightening line as tight as a tendon, swelling, pushing his insides toward some explosive climax. He inhaled, gripped the chair's arm, exhaled, trying to ride it out. Any minute now he would have to let go of the phone. He lifted his body a few inches off the seat and leaned forward, into the colossus.

Finally the pain broke and he jerked back, gasping for breath. The move was too quick. The swivel chair spun him head over heels. Relieved, he choked and laughed. He said her name once more, this time a roar. He heard the clang of bells, saw his feet fly up in the air as he hit the floor. Then everything went black.

Lena heard the crash and froze. The America she held in her head was full of cartoon violence with every story ending happily. This was different. It summoned up an East Berliner's response to calamity: Keep on walking. You saw nothing. It's not your business. With the wisdom of a girl raised behind the Wall, she knew that strangers in trouble could rarely be helped. The people who take care of trouble also tap your phone and keep their files up to date. To enter their web is to invite contamination by an unknowable virus.

Gustav agreed. A fearsome splay of barks exposed his alarm. Lena yanked his leash tight to silence him and started for the garden gate. A light next door went out.

The sudden darkness made her remember the cane. Flight temporarily stayed, she turned to look back. Now it was possible to see through the patio doors into the room where Hart had gone to answer the phone. He was still sitting in a chair, but the chair had fallen over backwards. She thought of an improvisation exercise her acting coach had assigned. Two people shared a bus seat in that same upended position. They had to pretend everything was normal, carry on conversation through twisted windpipes with their feet in the air. He looked absurd, calves dangling. His face was sunburn red.

She ran to his side, got down on her knees and said his name, but his eyes stared straight ahead, lips parted like a fish on land. She slapped his cheeks, nothing. Put two fingers to his throat, waited for a pulse, checking the beats against her nurse's watch. The rhythm was uneven. He was breathing, if just. His eyes were glassy. Gustav growled. She rubbed his throat, then pried the phone from Hart's hand. It was bleeping – busy. She pressed it off and on, found a dial tone and called the emergency number.

Why there was no trace of the young woman when the ambulance arrived is a question the actress could not have answered, but in any case, no one bothered to ask. As she had answered the door, they assumed she had made the call. The older of the two attendants recognised her immediately, and took time to compliment her work in the Academy Award-winning picture for which she was still remembered. He'd also seen her in a couple of made-for-TV dramas; his attention warmed the room. She told them everything she knew about the man who could not speak for himself. Without exactly lying, she held back on details that might have sparked more questions. She enjoyed playing the lead in the drama of Hart Granger's collapse.

Once they were out in the street, Lena began to run. Gustav followed, too well-trained to make a sound. As they broke into a sprint, his tongue slipped out between his teeth. He could have run like that all night. He hoped they were heading for damp woods, where they could catch their breath and keep on running away from the rank, unfamiliar smells of this unknown place. He was not a natural traveller. Cacophony meant danger. Unfamiliar smells were always bad. Only nature could restore the scent of security. But they did not come upon leaves. Instead, Lena drew him closer, holding the leash tight. She was a good runner. Usually, she could follow him to the brink of blissful rhythm but this time she slowed down too soon, yanked him into a well-lit doughnut shop. The tile floor smelled of chemical cleanser and the imprints of other beasts. They stood in line for a while, then she took a seat and dropped him a sweet morsel, which he swallowed in one bite.

Lena started to cry. Nothing that would attract attention, a few tears leaked out and were quickly wiped away. She sipped hot chocolate and gave Gustav the rest of her doughnut. In the distance she heard a siren, hoped it was the ambulance coming for Hart.

She regretted her decision to run. It was an impulse ingrained from an early age. Running meant she could never tell anyone what happened. A listener would want to know, did he recover or not? The lessons of prudence dictated silence. She looked down at Gustav, who was resting at her feet. He seemed to have forgotten already.

By the time she woke up the next morning, a tragic event had happened in New York City, in another time zone. When she came down for breakfast, the youth hostel staff and guests were gathered around a wide-screen television set in the lobby, watching what she thought at first was an action movie. A plane crashed into the side of a skyscraper, then another, and the buildings fell. Terrorists were bent on death and destruction, their own death and the destruction of America. As she watched the scene repeated throughout the day, she thought of her parents. If she called now, they would insist she come home. If she didn't call, they would suffer. She thought of Hart, lying feet up, maybe dead, and if so, missing a day that even on the day itself people said was momentous. His collapse seemed to fulfil her premonition that this day would somehow be significant. A beginning, an end, maybe both.

On the afternoon of September 11, when everyone else was transfixed by a public spectacle of terrorism, the actress was called to the L.A. Memorial Hospital to identify the body of the man who had arrived by ambulance, and passed away during the night. A fellow Canadian, his next of kin could not be reached. His mother was in a nursing home. His sister Amanda was attending a publishing conference in Beijing and, in the middle of a global crisis, couldn't get a flight into L.A. The actress was his only friend in California.

She glanced briefly at the corpse, felt sick, and turned away. His face was bloated, skin red and bruised. Almost beyond recognition, yet she knew it would be him. It must be him. Death changes the body instantly, she thought. Her word was believed by all.

In the days that followed Hart's death, the newspapers bulged with coverage of the disaster in New York. Nevertheless, the actress's agent succeeded in placing a small item in the *Los Angeles Times*, beside a flattering picture of his client taken in the soft shadows of late afternoon. The headline read, Actress Finds Screenwriter Dead.

Lena saw the report of Hart's demise as she and Gustav were waiting at the airport, bound for Berlin. She felt bad, as if by longing for an event to mark the fulcrum of her life, she had somehow willed his death. The side of her that could have been an actress saw the world in dramatic terms.

As the Lufthansa flight took off, she began to go over the details of the accident, step by step. She recalled how his racing pulse had been nearly normal, at least more or less what you'd expect of a healthy man who fell head over heals backwards in a swivel chair. His eyes were glassy, face red, but he had been breathing. She tried to remember a textbook chapter on shock, the various types and terms, but her memory was vague. She had not paid close enough attention. She wondered what more she might have done to help. Without thinking, she looked down at her nurse's watch and took her own pulse.

While the silver Pacific disappeared behind her, Lena Aurbach, the daughter of career bureaucrats and borderline hypochondriacs (hence their desire to steer her into nursing) realised that she knew a little but not nearly enough about the mysteries of the human body. She had not known how to pull a man back from the brink, the correct procedure during crisis.

She thought of an afternoon several years ago, when they'd come out of a café on Unter den Linden alle, where her mother liked to treat her to hot chocolate and a pastry, and found an old woman collapsed on the sidewalk. A man knelt at her side, taking her pulse. A few people slowed down but most walked briskly in the other direction, lifting their collars tight against the cold. Her mother pulled her away by the hand. "It's not our business," she said. "He's a doctor. There's nothing we can do."

At the time she had wanted no more than to stay and watch. Suddenly the memory seemed to mean something else. It struck Lena now that what is hidden cannot be revealed by the game of blindness. Unseen forces can sneak up and wreak havoc: New Yorkers running screaming toward the camera lens; people jumping to their deaths from a burning skyscraper; Hart slumped over, feet up and red-faced. In such cases, greater knowledge of procedure is necessary. Such knowledge required many more years of study.

By the time the aircraft reached the Atlantic Ocean, Lena had decided on a new future. If an old woman collapsed on a street or a man capsized, she would be the one to stop and kneel. Then if anyone tried to drag her away, she could break free and say, "I'm a doctor. I can help."

☞ III ☜

SANDRINE

Sandrine was the only woman Hart had ever loved, if the meaning of love can be stretched to include loyalty that wears many disguises. On the night he left her life forever, she was entertaining a colleague at home. Leonard Rosenthal: a recent junior appointment to the philosophy department at McGill University, tall with dark curly hair and perfect teeth, Lenny to his friends. He taught intermediate logic and a first-year survey course on central issues: the mind-body problem, freedom, scepticism and certainty, fate, time and the existence of God.

The second son of a real estate broker, Lenny graduated from Yale and bumped around the contract-lecturer circuit for a few semesters before wending his way back to Montreal where the Rosenthal family had deep roots. His grandfather, Lev, was a learned man who followed his more worldly brother from Gdansk in 1921. In the wake of an accident involving a rabid cat, Lev had married his deceased brother's widow, Rebecca, a natural beauty. They raised seven sons on St. Dominique Street, four of his own and three from the original alliance.

Lenny inherited both Rebecca's beauty and Lev's questing spirit. He won numerous scholarships, and while at Yale, had hoped to settle in the States. But getting back to Montreal had its attractions too. His tenure-track appointment closed the circle: a rabbi begets a professor of philosophy. If he couldn't believe in God, he could at least articulate the arguments for and against. He'd read about the Institute for Advanced Creative Dynamics, and was thrilled to meet its founder and director, who chaired the committee that hired him.

Out of gratitude for her help in steering him through the first stressful weeks in a new and important job, Lenny treated Professor Lamotte to an expensive dinner at Laloux. The food was excellent, the discussion lively. Afterwards, Sandrine invited him home for a cognac. With a fire crackling in the fireplace, Sandrine and Lenny settled into an ample tweed sofa that seemed to swallow them up. Gazing into her hazel eyes, he was on the verge of reaching for her neck to draw her lips to his, when the phone rang.

Sandrine's initial impulse was to ignore the call, but the answering machine was the old fashioned kind that broadcasts a caller's voice across the room, and she feared some intrusive message would spoil the mood. She'd been looking at Lenny's teeth which seemed unnaturally white, noticing too the taut outline of his pectoral muscles, how his shoulders seemed to fill out his lambswool sweater with a vitality that did the contributing beast proud.

Lenny was more than a decade younger than Sandrine. It pleased her immensely to watch his sexual eagerness spill out around the edges of conversation, seasoned with a charming hint of panic. It meant he still didn't know the answer to the night's big question, and cared very much. Not an ambivalent bone in his long, lanky body. She liked that. Needed it, even. Until the moment the phone rang, Sandrine Lamotte had been certain Leonard Rosenthal was the simple answer to a decade-long malaise that had hitherto proven impervious to therapy or distraction.

She said hello in a voice shot through with impatience. No one answered. Still, she knew who it was. Chagrin travelled up her spine and tightened the muscles in her jaw. What was there to say? *Yes, this is Sandrine, your long lost wife. Yes, I had your previous message about coming for a visit. I'm busy at the moment, good-bye.* Click.

But she said no such thing. Instead the telephone cord transmitted the sound of her breathing and returned the sound of his, like an umbilical link. They stayed like that for a few seconds, breathing at each other.

Hart and Sandrine met at a Mensa conference in Toronto the same year she published a paper weighing in on specific aspects of the mind/body question: Do we have minds and bodies? Can minds affect bodies? Is mind identical to body? As members of the world's leading association for individuals of certified high IQs, they had both laughed at the after-dinner speaker's joke about intelligent people being too smart for simple things like love. (More an ironic comment than repeatable joke, it had roused a ripple of nervous chuckles.) Soon enough they forgot the punch line, though the sentiment would haunt their liaison as it moved swiftly into marriage.

Hart admired, sometimes even envied Sandrine's devotion to her career. He worked hard, he played hard, but always with a shrug, as though nothing really mattered. Success and failure being no more than two sides of a coin, his only kick was the toss. As far as anyone knew, Hart's professional activities revolved around a series of quasi-creative adventures. He was often associated with the names of famous people, and always seemed to have money. Several ventures stretched over years, generated much talk and considerable publicity: the design and business plan of a proposed magazine, somewhere between *The New Yorker* and *Private Eye*, but catchier, taking more risks, available in remote parts of the planet; blueprints for a private resort in an undiscovered corner of Nepal, marketed exclusively to people like Hart; a consortium to build film studios in Dubai, where wealthy oil magnates would be teamed up with rigorously oddball talents to create radical and wildly lucrative erotic art-house films. And of course he played the market. Nobody was surprised when he gave up on creative schemes and turned his attention exclusively to the care and feeding of other people's money, through a partnership with a former tap-dancer-turned-salesman, Vince Bailey.

High-strung creatures with rigid personal habits, Sandrine and Hart had no patience with the quotidian issues of sharing space. They divorced in desperation after seven tempestuous years of irregular co-habitation. Lamotte versus Granger was a relatively calm dissolution. Nevertheless, the disentanglement of their mutual financial affairs required Hart to sell off a bundle of stocks, which had greatly increased in value during the time he quarrelled with Sandrine. It hurt, handing over all that cash, several hundred thousand dollars, especially knowing she would squirrel it away in low-yield bonds. He considered offering her investment advice, even went as far as drawing up a simple spreadsheet showing how she could turn her windfall into serious money.

But he got no further than a pre-lunch martini when it became clear that friendship with his ex-wife would have limits. Financial advice was out of bounds. Instead he bit his tongue and took his own advice. Six months later the market entered one of its famous spirals. Hart hung on and lost pretty well everything.

Normally, Sandrine didn't believe in the market but she did read the newspapers and stunned him at the time by suggesting that they take her half out of bonds and go shopping in the bear pit. Sandrine adored shopping. She had an instinct for bargains. The situation handed Hart a golden opportunity to demonstrate his financial prowess, thereby discovering what was fine about being divorced from a person like Sandrine: power struggles were no longer a temptation. All you had to do was wait for her to pitch, then swing the bat and run. Their mutually agreed-upon stock picks flew. Within a short time, he had paid back the loan, restored his own worth and given Sandrine a serious reserve to dignify her salary.

If people with high IQs are, as the joker claimed, too smart for love, they are not above the sin of pride. Friends privy to the riot of domesticity were stunned when, even as news of their separation was still making the rounds, Hart and Sandrine were seen dining together, filling symphony series seats, chatting amicably at a friend's annual New Year's party. Though unable to find their way through the simple tasks, they were determined to excel where ordinary mortals commonly founder. A mutual abhorrence for anything that smacked of failure led them to work at friendship, not that the terms or motives were ever made explicit. Sandrine said it would be nice to remain friends. Suddenly sad, Hart had agreed.

Those who noted the smooth transition predicted reconciliation, but it was not to be. Liberated from the tension of quarrelling, Sandrine plunged into work, publishing and travelling at a frantic pace, taking the IACD global, outstripping colleagues who were sucked into the swelter of home life, child-rearing and other time-consuming affairs. In professional circles, Dr. Lamotte was a fearsome success. A steady stream of densely argued journal articles poured forth; a second, more important book was announced and greeted with praise. Offers came from competing universities but Sandrine stayed loyal to McGill. Her reward was a mixture of icy awe tinged with pity from less dynamic colleagues. (Poor woman, they said, she still pines after her ex.)

Once divorced, Hart dated several beautiful and accomplished women, all of whom were encouraged to meet Sandrine. His stunning ex-wife never looked uncomfortable in the presence of his latest fling. Some people (mainly women) said Sandrine still had Hart by the balls, although others (mainly men) watched the parade with a twinge of envy. If he was unhappy, they had to admit, he hid it well.

Word of the ex-couple's financial collaboration leaked out, and Harvin Investments, Hart and Vince's investment consulting business, enjoyed a burst of new accounts. But the personal story left people confused. Couples who couldn't agree on what goes into the shopping cart were stunned to see Sandrine and Hart chatting happily together in public. For a time, the famous friendly divorce threatened to make a mockery of marriage.

And then it all fell gloriously apart. Those who'd had their doubts about the duration of an unstructured alliance were vindicated. An angry re-break-up was followed by reconciliation, then repeated, settling finally into a fiery routine.

Sandrine's much-talked-about surprise birthday party fit the pattern. A few weeks later, Hart put his possessions in storage, sublet his townhouse on Avenue de la Musée, and took off for Los Angeles to write a screenplay. Sandrine was seen with Lenny. How like Hart Granger to announce a risky creative venture in advance, they said. As if by deigning to try, he was guaranteed success in the film industry. And yet the move seemed somehow inevitable. Hart's life was nothing if not the raw material for something greater.

While Sandrine took the phone call, Lenny fled to the bathroom. Determined to hide out until she came looking for him, he examined the perfume bottles one by one, tiny expensive vessels with oil-encrusted necks, so many shapes, a bird, a lantern, a fat Buddha, sombre squares and a slender, blue urn with a frosted glass stopper. He sniffed them all, looking for the one she was wearing tonight.

The moment she'd slid into his car, a hazy waft of scent engulfed him like a promise. No female had ever inspired this level of carnal interest, at least not one he could recall at that moment. The idea of bedding a published scholar, a mature woman whose work he had been required to read as a graduate student, a woman almost old enough to be – Leonard knew better than to let his thoughts wander through archaic clichés. Yet he could not hide from himself the fact that Sandrine's age thrilled him. He wanted her because she was (still) beautiful, accomplished (in fact, his boss), and old enough to fully and profoundly appreciate the totality of what his carefully honed thirty-year-old body had to offer.

Finally, he found it, the tiny, unmarked jar, a pungent collision of ripe fruit and leather. Clamping his thumb to the opened neck, he tipped it once, and rubbed his damp thumb along the tips of his fingers. The scent struck him as the essence of Sandrine, as if she were standing right beside him naked. The aroma and the idea combined to produce movement in his crotch. He reached down to adjust his cock, and on an impulse, he rubbed it too, spreading the name-less perfume along his shaft until he couldn't stop and was forced to watch his red face in the bathroom mirror quiver with release.

Hart's wordless presence lasted thirty, maybe forty seconds, during which time Sandrine experienced a tumultuous mix-ture of worry, despair and anger. In the first few days fol-lowing his arrival in Venice Beach, he had phoned her three times. After that she'd heard nothing for weeks, until he called to invite her down for a visit. But he was never there when she called back to discuss the details. Then he left a message on her machine about how to get a taxi from the airport. Annoyed by his silence, outraged by his message, she could not give him the satisfaction of opening a conversa-tion. He had called her first. So she said nothing. She heard his breathing grow heavy. Seconds ticked by in which every-thing she hated about Hart including his passive-aggressive attachment to her goodness rose up and punctured the carefully constructed surface of their friendship. She wanted to scream. But remembering Lenny might hear through the bathroom door, she said evenly, "Why did you call?"

"Sandrine!" His voice was thin with urgency. He said nothing. Instead, she heard a crash. Shuffling, footsteps, rustling, choking. A dog barking furiously.

Then she thought she heard a woman's voice, and slammed down the phone, picked it up again immediately, but the line was dead.

As she held the phone to her ear, the dial tone gave way to the ebb and flow of tides, captured in a seashell. Thousands of miles away, she could still hear him breathing, pictured him standing on the beach at night, staring out at an awesome Pacific horizon. Glancing at her watch, the diamond-studded Cartier he had given her for her fortieth birthday, she realized it was still early in Los Angeles. A woman at his side, Hart would be gazing at swaths of pink and purple stretched across the horizon, like a sunset on Fiji. They had vacationed there in the dead of winter, shortly after the divorce. A spontaneous week on his frequent flyer points, lazy days and nights punctuated by boozy, friendly sex, no discussion. Sandrine had thrown herself into paradise with all the care and enthusiasm at her disposal. She rode him with her eyes open, avoiding his, giving away nothing. Hart surpassed himself. Out of the corner of her eye, she had caught his surprise, and was pretty sure he was close to a melt down. She longed to bend down and kiss him on the lips, stroke his fleshy cheeks and whisper a declaration of eternal love. But the risk was too great. Affection was not part of the planned performance. The victory of his surprise was too precious to be threatened by a kiss. So she closed her eyes and when it was over, slipped out to the bathroom. He was asleep when she returned.

"Are you all right?" Lenny was standing beside her, flushed, smelling of fresh perfume and faintly of sweat. He had heard her shriek, and found her sitting on the floor, holding the phone.

"Yes, fine. I just had a strange call." She struggled awkwardly to get up, Lenny offering a hand. He was waiting for an explanation.

She pressed Hart's number on the speed-dial. Now the line was busy. She programmed the phone for automatic redial and took deep gulps of air, holding onto the table for ballast. Was Hart dead? Logically, her philosopher's mind counselled, nothing is certain. A few noises, his desperate cry, a busy signal. Not much to go on. Yet she knew he was gone. The idea surged through her body like an electric current, leaving her stiff and light.

"My ex-husband Hart. He's in L.A . . . . I'm sure he'll call back if it's important." Then she placed the receiver back in its cradle.

Lenny nodded, perfectly willing to drop the subject. "Can I get you a drink?"

Her eyes blazed. She reached out, put a hand on his shoulder, a gesture that reminded him strangely of the way his old high school football coach used to greet players coming off the field. But then, in swift contradiction, she reached for his mouth and kissed him hungrily. They kissed until she pulled him down on to the carpet and undid his belt buckle, following the scent, her own scent. Legs flailing, groaning, groping at buttons and writhing, they dove in together, as if they had a train to catch.

Lenny was only marginally surprised. This was, after all, more or less what he'd intended. But it was happening so quickly. He threw himself into the moment, spirit willing but flesh (all things considered) somewhat taken aback.

Sandrine read his hesitation as shyness and was deeply touched. With a burst of enthusiasm she had not felt since Fiji, she threw herself into the seduction of Leonard Rosenthal; he responded fervently with all the moves that came to mind.

Afterwards, she lay back on the Persian carpet and closed her eyes. Lenny sat up, breathless and proud.

"I'll get the drinks," he said.

"Thank you," she sighed. And wondered immediately if he would misunderstand.

After he'd gone home, she poured herself a nightcap and called the L.A. police department. There was no news. The scent of Lenny lingered. The flesh between her legs was sore. She closed the drapes, took a sleeping pill with a cup of hot milk, unplugged the phone and climbed into bed.

It was late afternoon the next day before the police called back to say Hart Granger was dead. She offered to fly down and identify the body, but was told that would not be necessary. The woman next door had taken charge. Next of kin had already been notified.

She sat all day, alone and dazed, in front of the TV, watching a new world unfold in full-colour horror.

Next of kin. A few hours earlier, hearing herself excluded from a phrase like that would have caused offence. Instead, she felt an odd surge of relief. I am not a widow, she thought. No, I am not Hart's next of kin.

❧ IV ❧

KITTY

The cotton sheet rubs against Kitty Granger's knees while she sleeps, leaving sores. She shifts position. Something hard in the mattress, a spring or a wrinkle of cloth, pokes her thighs. She cries out, "Ouch." Every joint aches, a niggling litany of pains that come and go without warning, the mind smothered in complaints from a worn-out body, time frittered away on fussing. But there are worse fates, she knows. The muddled, drooling sentence of senility would be worse.

On a bad day, she grits her teeth and fixes her attention on a single, vivid thought to be turned over, followed through in the next clear patch of lucidity. So much to think about, so few good days. Raising her head from the pillow, she looks around the room, sees that no one has heard her cry and sinks back, relieved. The slightest grievance can bring on some new medication, leading to fog or sleep, a further waste of time.

Across the room, a lump lies hidden under blankets. She can tell it's a man by the wheezing spurts and rasps of breath, intimate male sounds, volcanic and foolish. The nurses say, no, this is the ladies' floor. She suspects they've been told to lie by the management of St. Joachim's, a beige, sick-smelling place, somewhere awful in New York. It was Amanda's decision, bringing her down to the States, stuffing her in with strange men and Catholics. That's what comes of marrying one! In no uncertain terms, Kitty had outlined her views to the lady in the next bed, but now that bed is empty.

The windows are sealed shut, the air is hot and stale. Grasping a corner of the sheet, she begins the laborious task of uncovering her legs. It takes hours and never fails to cause a stir, the sight of a small, immobile lump of bones wrapped in paper skin, naked and exposed. The nurses cannot fathom why a naturally modest woman would insist on removing her clothes. *She'd be mortified if she knew.*

Kitty keeps her eyes shut and listens to their talk. In the corner of her brain that struggles to manage pain, she knows very well who draws those sheets away, and why: for the pleasure of revenge on the ravaged body that is holding down her mind.

The stroke damaged her power of speech, but her mind she is sure remains clear and furious. Without the power to respond or interrupt, she is deluged by one-way conversations fit for an idiot. Dear this, dear that, pointless chatter full of coos and kisses. Only Amanda still bothers to articulate. She has moved Kitty to a nursing home near her office, so she can come in every day to read from the newspapers and drop off new books on tape. Kitty takes to words like exercise, determined to keep her mental muscles firm and up to the tasks of memory. A faithful daughter is a blessing, she concedes, even one who tends to lecture: "You were a crackerjack nurse, Mum. Remember? Why not give these girls a smile? Tell them they're doing a good job."

Kitty pretends not to hear, but after Amanda leaves, she savours the picture of herself as a young nurse, sitting with the others on their break, drinking coffee, smoking, clucking tongues and yes, of course, telling jokes on the cranky ones. Before she was Mrs. Dr. Terrance Granger, she'd been one of them, so cocky and sure they would never turn into old crows, helpless bores with nothing to do but wait. She had not known then, so can hardly blame these young girls now: the old do not lie idle, waiting for death like teatime. Dying isn't waiting. It is work. Before extinction comes recollection, a duty to remember, a story to be told to the end.

Summer, 1945. A small white house in a quiet Montreal neighbourhood, Notre-Dame-de-Grace – N D G to its stolid Anglo inhabitants who are uncomfortable with foreign-sounding names.

On her way out to the garden, Kitty Woodhouse slams the screen door shut, a gesture aimed at Ellen, who is sitting at the kitchen table, crying into a handkerchief embroidered with violets. A terrible disgrace has fallen on the Woodhouse family. It is Kitty's doing, yet her mother suffers shame as though the fault were hers alone.

Frank's portion of the shame is tainted by ambivalence. Siding with his wife, he damns the brute who did this to their only child, but the act itself arouses something akin to admiration. Try as he might, Frank Woodhouse cannot fully embrace the link between fecundity and shame. At night, when his wife has fallen asleep in her tears, he lies awake wondering, when and where did this happen? Under his own roof? Were they swept up, carried away by an urgent, unstoppable force? These questions make his blood race. His thoughts are free of judgement but when morning comes, he will fix a look of resignation on his face, prepared to obey the rules of humiliation.

Kitty rejoices in the slam, heads for the garden, climbs into the double-sided swing built by her father and freshly painted every other spring. With one foot, she gives the ground a push, leans back against the wooden slats and settles into the familiar rhythm of summer. An ocean sky of clouds calls for wishes. She offers up Neil Roberts, twenty-two, tall and gorgeous, with black hair and a wicked sense of humour. Her heartfelt wish is to see Neil sitting at the dining room table, telling one of his stories. Ellen will resist at first but then her famous rippling laugh will catch hold and carry her off. It doesn't happen often, but when something strikes her funny bone, there is no more beautiful woman on earth, and it's easy then to forget how often and how easily she cries. Kitty wishes they could pay someone to make her mother laugh, but there's a war on. Money is tight, parental laughter is in short supply. As the swing glides high into the noontime sun, defying the gravity of events, she is as sure as she can be that Neil will see her through, that any minute now, he will roll into the driveway in the Chevy, open the passenger's door and take her away from a cheerless house where no one ever, ever tells a joke.

Only years later will it dawn on Kitty that her mother knew all about Neil and the famous blue Chevrolet, which belongs on the car lot and isn't his at all. It is one of the reasons she is crying. She cannot abide giving her only child to a used car salesman's feckless son. She is English, a member of a family that puts great store in who one is and what one does, details that creep out between the lines of letters from abroad. When she was Kitty's age, she cast her lot with a man whose dreams did not come true. But she knows better now. She is not prepared to sit idly by while more mistakes are made. From now on, Ellen will insist on dignity, synonymous with comfort, and not just a brave face worn to cover despair.

In the weeks that follow Kitty's announcement, nothing goes as planned. True to her wishes, Neil pulls up outside the house, but he is quickly sent away. When the telephone rings, Ellen gets there first. Finally, it stops ringing. Kitty howls, pleads, threatens to run away, but mostly she sleeps, each day, a small surrender. Long evenings and empty afternoons yield finally to the time zones of pregnancy, where the past is a fairy tale, the present, a heavy swoon. She pins her hopes on a distant future, sometime after a dreadful, sweet delivery when she can return to real time. *Only X-more days away.* By the fifth month, she is too numb to worry about where Neil has gone, and too tired to care.

No one at St. Jo's is allowed to escape the mid-morning snack tray of biscuits, fruit and tea. Kitty hears the approaching cart, and groans at the rude, unwelcome break from reverie. As the duty nurse tucks a fresh pillow behind her head and rattles on about the weather, she is surprised to learn it is snowing outside. She had thought the season was summer. Then she remembers: the season of her memory was summer. By the time the tea tray disappears, she is alone again, ready to drift back to the garden where by now the leaves have fallen.

A crisp November day, her suitcases are packed. Frank waits in the front room, overcoat buttoned, hat in hand, while she looks out once more over the frozen grass and gives the dog a good-bye hug. She is glad to be on the move, excited by the prospect of new landscapes and people she does not know.

Gripping a suitcase in each hand, Frank leads her to Windsor station on the bus. His shoulders sag; he wheezes and stumbles on a crack in the pavement. Beside him, Kitty feels bulky and strong. She tries to take a suitcase, but he refuses. For weeks, he has treated her like expensive china, hardly speaking above a whisper.

This journey is the first time they've been alone in months. She tries to read her father's thoughts, but his face is blank. Does he blame her? Despise her? Is he heart-broken or angry? Will he ever forgive, or at least forget? Her mother's arc was clear. Tears and shouts gave way to muted phone calls; plans were made and quietly announced. Kitty listened with her eyes shut, knowing there was no way forward but to slip back into childhood, obey, and wait. Frank stayed in his workshop, making birdcages.

On the Amtrak platform, he sets down the suitcases and checks his pocket watch, sputtering about the cold. Kitty fishes in her purse for the ticket, and when she looks up, their eyes meet. This time he does not shy away. His gaze is sad, as though he believes she will be gone forever.

She is tempted to say, I'm sorry. So sorry I have made you suffer. Hatred of Ellen had kept her strong, but now, confronted by wordless love, she crumbles.

"Oh, Daddy . . ."

He shakes his head.

The porter heaves her suitcases into the railway car, and tells her to get aboard. Frank's shoulders slump. "She's to get off in Sherbourne, down in Vermont," he murmurs gravely. "You'll tell her when it's her stop?"

The porter winks at Kitty. "Is she deaf? If not, she'll hear the announcement."

"No, I'll be fine." She smiles, grateful for an exchange that is not tainted by the unmentionable presence in her womb.

Before Frank can think of what to say, she dusts his cheek with a kiss and disappears into the train. The whistle blows. These last few minutes should pass quickly. But nothing goes as planned.

Alone on the platform, Frank scans the windows for a last glimpse of his daughter. She is nowhere to be seen. For weeks he has been paralysed in her presence, caught up in the lugubrious spell of Ellen's disappointment. Now her absence shatters the spell, and he is galvanised. He knows exactly what to say and do.

He climbs on board the train and plants himself in the seat next to hers. She whispers a protest but he stays rigid. The whistle blows, final call. She is frantic, "Daddy, please!"

The porter rushes forward, demanding Frank get off the train, this instant. Frank is beyond reasoning. He folds his arms, stares straight ahead. The train lurches forward. The porter shouts.

Then Frank is standing in the aisle, arms flailing. Possessed by a memory of the night she was born, he is ready to fight. The midwife had done her level best to keep him away, but Frank put his foot down, stayed by the bed and held Ellen's hand throughout. He saw the whole bloody ordeal from beginning to end. He knows what lies ahead, knows more than his child. He will not abandon her.

The porter grabs at his arms, takes an elbow in the nose. Blood spurts out, but they are moving, chugging, inching forward toward the light. Victory! He will be there when the time comes, to hold her hand.

Suddenly, a jolt, they are thrown forward. Three thick men in uniforms clutch at his arms. The train has stopped. It inches back into darkness, stops again, and the men drag Frank away, leaving him on the platform as the car door slams shut. The train begins to move. He goes limp, does not think to buy a ticket, or follow her on the next train. He will regret this moment forever.

Through tears, he finds Kitty, her face framed by the window, both hands pressed against the glass. She gazes at a crumpled little man standing still and alone. She does not want him to follow. She smiles, and waves goodbye. Blows him a kiss, and is gone.

A miracle, and yet Kitty isn't one bit surprised. When she opens her eyes, Neil is sitting at the side of her bed. Her first thought is, Terrance will be furious. But no, all that was before. Terrance knows nothing about Neil, about what happened in Vermont.

The appearance of Neil Roberts after so many years sends her spinning. She is delirious with joy. So many questions, her mouth is dry. Dark-haired Neil, his bulky frame too big for the folding chair. He looks as though he has been sitting there for hours, waiting for her to wake up. She says his name but the sound remains inside her head. Still, he smiles, leans forward. His lips move but the words drift by out of reach. She cannot bring her mind to bear on the sense of what he says.

She gives up trying, instead turns her attention to the task of lifting her head off the pillow. She can see his manly hands are wrapped around hers, which are small, wizened. She is old and Neil is still so young. How can this be? It's unfair. She is tempted to call out for Terrance, but that seems all wrong. The effort of trying to sit up makes her neck hurt. She settles back into the pillow, closes her eyes, and realises too late that this was a mistake. Now they will not open. Yet the image of Neil burns fresh. She feels his hand gripping hers. She calls his name, over and over. She has so much to tell him. The whole story, a lifetime, and so many questions.

Where have you been? What kept you?

She would like to ask about the car. Of all the many things Ellen said to break her down, put an end to foolish hopes, the worst concerned the Chevy. Ellen said Neil's father had given it to him, told him to take it, drive off, get some air. So he'd gone, no one knew where. Kitty left two phone messages with Neil's mother and wrote to him, a typewritten envelope sent in care of the dealership. Not a word came back.

She decided her mother was lying. Neil never saw her letter. Still, he wasn't stupid. He had a knack for getting what he wanted. Surely Neil would have known how to find her, no matter what. If he'd wanted to find her. Doubts spun like webs, filled her days with longing and regret.

As one week folded into the next, she began to accept that months, maybe even years must pass before their paths would cross again. In the limbo of Vermont, she learned patience. By the time her own clothes fit again, she had stopped thinking about the distant future, or the past. The baby was a boy. She looked at him once, slipped a paper bearing Neil Roberts' name between the folds of his blanket, and left it at that. If the woman who got him had any sense, she'd take the hint and know the baby's name must be Neil. A son will someday go looking for his father, she was sure.

The return trip to Montreal bore none of the sobs and sighs of departure. The snow had started to melt. Frank had a new job working evenings and couldn't meet her train, so she walked home from the station. Ellen offered cake and did her best to smile. The front hall was filled with boxes. The house had been sold. They were moving into an apartment in another neighbourhood, with new neighbours who would not wonder were Kitty had been all winter, or why.

In September, Kitty started her nurse's training. Two years later she met Terrance, and put it all behind her.

When she opens her eyes again it is the quiet part of the night. The chair beside her bed is empty but the space occupied by Neil still glows, a halo image, as if he has just this second left. All her aches and pains are gone. Her mind is clear, like the summer air after a rain.

Then it hits her, she has seen Neil before, and not so long ago. A crowd of strangers, a yellow room, some kind of party, but where? When was it? The faces are familiar, the room itself is not. She looks for the button on a wire, intending to ring the nursing station and tell them to call Amanda. She'll remember, she was there too. She would know if this is real, or just a dream like all the other dreams of Neil. The picture in her mind's eye is vivid, a yellow room, a dark-haired man bending down to whisper in Amanda's ear. How could that be – Neil and her child, Amanda? Suddenly the pieces fall into place and she knows it was not Neil Roberts who whispered into Amanda's ear, it was the baby, grown into a man.

She had still been living in her own home and had contact with the world when a letter arrived, postmarked Vermont. An 'attorney' writing on behalf of his 'client' who was seeking permission to correspond . . .

Legal letters normally bring bad news. How her hands had trembled as she tore it open. At first she did not understand. Then she did, and was momentarily gripped by an old fear that had haunted her for years. Someone would discover the awful secret, and blame her. But it didn't matter any more. All those who cared were dead. She read the letter over, and cried, read it a dozen times and cried for days until finally there was only one thing left to do. She wrote back: *Yes, tell him he can see me. I live alone.* Months passed. She heard nothing. Disjointed dreams of Neil, Frank and Ellen crowded every night, and then she had a stroke.

The digital clock flashes 4:17. Kitty looks away. She is curled up on the edge of the bed, one arm pinned between the sheet and her ribcage, an awkward position. Before long the breakfast tray will come clanking into the room, steamrolling privacy. The minute changes to 4:18. The time for reverie has run out.

Her eyes light on the steel, grey folding chair. No halo now, only an empty chair. So the boy Neil has come and gone?

Her heart is numb. Thoughts soar and dip like white birds, falling stars.

An empty chair is a dead chair. Amanda said Hart died, but that isn't possible, he's too young. Amanda always loved stories. She often gets things wrong. Hart would not be dead yet. Hart can be counted on to carry on. He is so much like Terrance, although they never got along, of course not. Both so stubborn when it came to the simplest things, full of dreams but ungenerous in ways that count. Such as explanations. Terrance never gave Hart enough credit. Living with those two was like walking on eggshells. Mother was hard but Daddy understood. All the same, there is a drop of Frank Woodhouse in Hart: the silent type who weeps when tears are called for.

She looks down at her legs, blue white in the creeping dawn. At two hands resting like empty gloves on bare knees. Who is this, she wonders? Old legs on an old woman? An unfamiliar suitcase left somewhere, out of mind? She does not feel old now, she's beyond all that. She would not have known what to say to the boy-man-Neil. It is enough to know he found his way.

The pain starts at the back of her neck, moving swiftly like an eclipse of the moon. Her skull throbs, shoulders slump. She leans forward, sits on the edge of the bed, empty of regret, lighter now that a life-long secret is no more. A second wave, she yields. She is young and old in the same instant, a rebellious daughter full of hope and an old woman, finally beyond the reach of guilt and fear. No time left. Others will have to carry on.

As she falls, pain is replaced by light. The last picture is a room, precise, familiar, a place of celebration with brocade wallpaper and mirrors. Three children are sitting side by side around a table lit by candles. No longer sweet babies, they are cagey, clever, all grown up. Hart's lips burn with a sharp remark. Amanda is smiling sweetly, telling a story she hopes will lift the mood. Neil listens, bows his head. The three of them are holding hands. The light grows unbearably white then disappears.

❧ V ❧

WANDA

Wanda Springer is worried about her husband Neil. Worry gnaws at her like the symptoms of disease, except that in this case there are no odds and no known treatment. The problem lies with Neil, a fifty-five-year-old welder, a sports-minded father of three. To the best of Wanda's knowledge, in twenty-odd years of marriage Neil has never looked twice at another woman. But he's involved in something now that could well wreak similar havoc, maybe worse. In desperation, she confided the whole story to her friend Marie, who's been through a few cyclones herself. Marie said there's nothing to be done but wait and pray he'll come around. So Wanda prays. The trouble is she doesn't know what to pray for. Marie says, pray for patience and luck. Patience, fine, but what would this luck look like? Will the clocks roll back? Does someone have to die?

The situation began last May, although it dates back virtually to 1979, the summer Wanda and Neil found each other. Two worn-down souls fell in love and got married, a quick succession of events powered by a love that neither of them doubted for a minute. From the very beginning, they agreed on what they wanted from life and even more surely, what they did not want – trouble. The kind you look for, invite into the nest and later regret. It's not as if they were young. At thirty-three, Neil had already lost one woman to fool-ishness and dated a long line of disasters. Wanda was thirty with a bad marriage behind her and nothing from childhood to suggest that happiness was something you could count on.

The night she spilled out her story to Marie, they were sitting in a coffee shop across from the YM-YWCA sharing a bran muffin, a ritual after their weekly aerobics class. They'd set themselves the goal of losing thirty pounds each before Christmas, the prize (or penalty) being one hundred dollars, payable to the one who got there first, or came closest. Wanda had not intended to go on and on. She mentioned simply that Neil had gone up to Montreal with the Rotary Club and come back with some fairly strange news: he has a whole family up there and he might even be Canadian.

She did not come right out with the worst of her fears, that this bump in the road was more like a ninety-degree turn after which the life they'd built up together would change beyond recognition. But Marie must have suspected some-thing. She said, "Listen honey, let's call home and say we're going for a drink. I think you deserve it."

Weakened already by the drug of confession, Wanda agreed, though her friend's sympathy made her queasy. She'd have almost preferred the brush-off. When someone like Marie insists on hearing the whole story, you can figure it must be serious. They went to a bar two blocks from the Y parking lot where the carpet smelled of stale beer. A night baseball game was showing on a big-screen TV. Marie chose a booth near the window so the cheer of the crowd and the advertising jingles could not penetrate their conversation. Plates of nachos and fries were delivered to tables circling the game, but in deference to their winter diet, the women kept to white wine spritzers.

This is more or less what Wanda said to Marie:

All the while I was going with Neil, I thought, this is too good to be true. We met at one of those singles' clubs where you expect the worst. Right from the start Neil was calm and in control, interested but not one bit pushy. He just came right up and asked me to dance. That was it. A week after we met, he took me home to meet Esther and Ted (his folks). I said to him on the way back, Neil, they're great people. Warm, funny, open, they don't pry or get on your nerves. They look at you when you're talking. I just love them! You are so lucky. And I was thinking, too good to be true.

As if he read my mind, Neil says, "They aren't my real parents."

I say, "What?"

"I'm adopted."

"But they brought you up?"

"Sure," he says. "I have no other memories."

So I say, "Then they're your *real* parents. They brought you up." And I'm thinking, they are why you are a perfectly loveable human being. (As you know, I didn't have that kind of upbringing myself. By the time Neil came along, I was looking hard, eyes wide open, ready for a chance to put my past behind me.) So, we got married, had three kids, and I'll tell you, there is nobody more surprised than Wanda Bell Springer that we were able to be the kind of parents that Ted and Esther were. Salt of the earth, those two. They were role models for me, Marie. People you could always look up to.

Sure, at first all the religion business kind of made me wince, because I didn't have it as a kid, and when you come to it as an adult, it can seem a little strong. Witnessing, preaching, the whole show. Compared to the outside world. But I said to myself, if this is what it takes to turn my life around, then fine. Faith isn't always a bolt of lightening, you know. It grows on you. It took a few years but I have faith now. It's me, my true self. I believe deeply that the Lord watches over his flock and that prayer is a powerful instrument. Everything happens for a reason.

When the kids were small, we spent all our time trying to get enough sleep and keep the bills paid. We were looking forward to a day when we'd have time for ourselves. Neil used to talk about the trips we'd take. Once they were on their own, we'd have time for each other. That was our plan.

Two years ago, Esther died. A few months afterwards Neil decided to look into what he calls his 'birth' mother. It wasn't my place to comment. Though I'll tell you, every bone in my body said, do not do this. It will serve no purpose. Honour thy father and thy *real* mother, the one who gave you mothering. Leave it at that.

He swore it wouldn't change a thing. "I would just like to know." That's what he said.

So, he hired an agency and they came back a few weeks later with some woman's name up in Montreal. He didn't tell me much, just her name. Kitty. I didn't ask for details. I thought, if he needs to talk, he will. I did not have a good feeling, even then. Sorry to say, but I almost wished we'd lost Ted and not Esther. Neil would never have dared open that can of worms if Esther'd been alive. He loved that woman and she deserved every drop of the love and respect he gave.

At first, knowing the so-called birth mother's name seemed to be enough. Months went by and he said nothing. Then all of a sudden he announced his Rotary Club was going up to Montreal on a convention, it would have been last May. For Neil this was practically a sign from the Lord. His mother was calling him! He wanted me to go along. I said, "Nope, you are on your own."

I would say it was, if not a fight, at least a strong difference of opinion. Over and over, the same thought kept running through my mind: let sleeping dogs lie. Don't push yourself on her. If you ask me, that woman must have had her reasons for what she did. Back in those days, girls didn't have the options they do now. Or the choices.

Well damn her reasons, Marie! I don't care about her. But I do care about my husband. I don't want him to get hurt. I told him to his face: to go up there and confront her is to let yourself in for a powerful hurt. As a woman, I know. Which is why I did my level best to hold him back, even if it looked real bad on me, and it did. Real bad. I was one mean-mouthed bitch for weeks before he went. For his own sake, because goddamn it I love him! Anyway, he went.

He found her, all right. Don't ask me how. When Neil wants something, he knows how to get it. Turns out she'd had a stroke. She was confined to a wheelchair, barely sensible. You can't rush up on an old woman, he says. So he didn't even introduce himself, just put in an appearance and left. He said no more. I didn't pry.

A couple of weeks later, a letter arrives with snapshots from his half-sister Amanda, her husband Tom, and their two kids, who live in New York City. Then it all comes out, how he met practically the whole family at some kind of party up in Montreal. Only then does he mention a sister! Anyway, she tells him all about how Kitty's folks were English, they came over to Montreal before the Second World War. There's a brother too, named Hart. Amanda wants to reunite the family. So she invites us all to New York. Not a flicker of shock, as if it was all perfectly normal! Your mother has a child out of wedlock and fifty-five years later he turns up at the door!

I haven't been to NYC since my stepfather took me there in 1965 and that was not a good time. But I was not going to miss this. So last summer, we went. They put us up in a hotel, a few blocks from their fancy apartment right off Central Park. Amanda got tickets for a Broadway play and of course the kids loved that. Her husband is a lawyer and as tall as Neil. I have to say most of the conversation went on between Neil and Amanda. I played the wallflower, though she did her best to cover it up. We'd be walking along the street and she'd take me by the arm. We don't do that kind of thing back where I'm from, we don't kiss hello and goodbye, which is a shame. We probably should show our feelings more. Still, every time she talked to me it was like she had to remind herself I was there. I kept looking at her husband to see if he noticed anything but he was too wrapped up in the kids. Of course, they loved the attention. Over the whole two-day trip, I doubt Neil and me made eye contact more than twice.

I kept my cool, though. Hard to believe, but I did. Finally it was over. We got in the car to come home and I was glad I hadn't been the least bit frosty.

As soon as we pulled away, Neil says, "Isn't she something?"

I did not comment, just leaned my head back and pretended to sleep. Three pairs of ears in the back seat, I was not about to spill my guts out. But I can tell you, I felt sick to my stomach. Neil Springer is blind in love with his sister. I mean that in the worst possible sense.

By now their glasses were empty. The waiter came over and Marie said she had to be going, but Wanda insisted on ordering one more round, hold the soda. Marie said she didn't know Neil that well, but he was highly respected in Rotary circles and an active Christian. She doubted very much if meeting his birth mother, or a half-sister, was going to affect his responsibilities as a father and husband. Then why the secrets, Wanda demanded? Why didn't he mention a sister as soon as he got back from Montreal? Marie said, he's just being careful. If she'd rejected him, he wouldn't necessarily have wanted anybody to know.

"Not even his own *wife*?"

"Some men are like that," Marie offered. Have faith, she said. But Wanda wasn't listening. Instead, she launched into a full account of Neil's smitten state, how he hardly listened to a word she said, his puppy dog plans to get the two families together again as soon and as often as possible – skiing in the Canadian mountains was the latest. On her third glass of wine, she confessed that since his trip to Montreal, things hadn't been great in the warmth department. Whatever happened in bed was at Wanda's instigation and reeks of a chore, like hand-pumping water at the cottage. From that point on, Marie realised she just had to let Wanda talk. And talk she did:

Sometimes he wakes up in the middle of the night in a sweat, and I know he's dreaming of her. I say fine, get it over with, go after her. Screw your brains out. Do it right in front of my nose. Clear the air. I'm sorry, really, Marie, I'm so sorry. Why'd I ever let you talk me into telling you all this with liquor on the table? This is liquor talking. And stress. A great deal of stress. More than I've got the time or energy for. Ask the waiter to bring me a coffee. Then I'm going home and you're going to forget that last bit, because I don't mean it. I love my husband. I'm strong enough to ride it out. I pray for distance, that's right, distance from the whole thing. Just step back, get it in perspective. My husband is getting to know his sister. She's a married woman with two great kids and if I may say so, a very attractive husband who seems completely unaware of what is going on. Well, he's a New York lawyer. Need I say more? Okay, I'll be honest, that's part of the problem. The way Tom looks at Neil, I know he's laughing at the whole thing, at Neil and me. At the way Neil worships Amanda. A couple of small town hicks craning their necks along the streets of Montreal and New York, and Christ almighty, next summer we're all going to Cape Cod!

. . .

What's she look like? Well Marie, a question like that does not put me at ease. Because it means you consider her a woman! And she is his SISTER! It is against the law in America to go after your sister.

. . .

Okay, sorry. She is very, very beautiful. Even my own kids, when they met her for the first time, they could not stop looking. She's slim and small, with blond hair and well I'd say she isn't even aware that she's drop dead gorgeous. Apparently she was sickly as a child but she's fine now. Remember that time we saw Julia Roberts up close? And we said, ha-ha, crow's feet. Great lights needed here, babe? Well, you don't say that about Amanda. You say: she is a miracle. My husband is in love with a miracle. You know what's worse? She looks at him like he's a miracle. There you go. The biggest disaster of my life, and I thought I'd had a few.

. . .

Okay, now, say something that'll make me feel better.

Wanda didn't turn up for the Tuesday night aerobics class the following week. Marie intended to give her a call but kept putting it off. Then she sprained her wrist and missed a few weeks herself. When she got back to class, Wanda was nowhere to be seen. Just before Christmas Marie ran into Neil at the mall and felt a wave of guilt.

There he was, heading up a fund-raising campaign for the Vermont families who'd lost someone in 9/11. His group had come out with a full line of t-shirts, mugs and bumper stickers bearing the slogan Live Free in America or Else, with proceeds going to the grieving families. She made a point of going over to the kiosk where he was manning the cash register. She even bought a set of stars and stripes placemats so he wouldn't think she was interfering when she casually asked about Wanda. Neil's face clouded.

"I don't know what's gotten into her," he sighed. "To be honest, I'm mystified. Sure wish you'd give her a call."

Marie looked at him closely. She was about to ask what he meant, but just then a delegate from the police force came over to congratulate Neil on all he'd done on behalf of the victims. She could see he wanted to have that conversation, so she said her goodbyes and stood at a distance, watching him nod and smile. It struck her then that people like Neil keep America ticking, but all too often the charitable types fall down when it comes to doing good at home. Still, she didn't think Neil was the kind to be swept away by hopeless love. If anything, he'd add to the family nest. But it wouldn't be like him to get carried away, or take a risk.

First thing the next day, she called Wanda. Her friend's voice on the phone sounded thick and hazy, as if she spoke through a drug. They agreed to meet for a coffee.

Marie arrived early and ordered a piece of cherry cheese-cake. She ate quickly, thinking she might pay right away and avoid having to admit that she'd slipped from her New Year's resolution, even though the urge to eat something sweet and rich felt less like common indulgence than a desperate antidote to dread. She was not looking forward to this meeting.

At the sight of Wanda Springer walking through the restaurant door, Marie dropped her fork. Wanda had reached her desired goal, all right, and gone right on by. Looked like she was wearing somebody else's tracksuit; it hung forlornly on her shrunken body. Her face was grey. Her hands shook when she pulled out a package of cigarettes and lit up.

"This is the non-smoking section," Marie pointed out. They never smoked after class, as a tribute to self-control.

"Fuck it," Wanda said, and struck a match. From that moment on, Marie had to force herself to stay seated, so badly did she want to avoid hearing what her friend was determined to say:

Neil's mother died. His so-called 'real' mother. The one who gave him up for adoption right after he was born. We all went up for the funeral. Montreal in January, I'll tell you Marie, we have nothing to complain about down here. Wind so cold it felt like swallowing knives. Neil loved it. He said it made him think of hockey. He took a week off work and insisted we see the sights. I said, you have a very odd way of grieving, Mr. Springer. He said, she was an old woman whose time had come. Thank God we had a chance to know her before she went.

We? Ha. I never clamped eyes on the bitch. Wouldn't have, even if he offered to introduce us. Am I the only one who feels loyalty to Esther, the woman who loved him and took him in and brought him up to be a God-fearing responsible man? An American, for Christ's sake! Let's not lose sight of that. He is a blue-blood American and so are his three *natural* children, though it seems to me he is doing everything in his power to pry them away from their fortunate heritage. He took them out of school to attend the funeral of a grandmother they had never known, and then he forced them to skate. And after all that's happened, 9/11 and all that! I stayed in the hotel, contented myself with laps and weights. I swear I have never felt more American than I did up there, sitting in the Holiday Inn thinking about them mopping up flesh and bones from under the Twin Towers. I'll tell you, it gives you a certain perspective. Takes my breath away to see how fragile we are. How very, very fragile. And it isn't over yet, Marie. This thing that's hit us, it isn't over.

Marie wasn't sure whether Wanda was talking about her personal crisis or the threat of international terrorism. She was afraid to ask. As far as she could follow Wanda's reasoning, there didn't seem to be any difference. She kept mouthing phrases they'd both heard on Sunday morning TV. The end of the world as we know it. Threat to peace and liberty. Homeland security.

She was sure Wanda was going to start crying any minute. So obvious was the depth of her despair that even the waitress noticed and ignored her second cigarette. But she did not cry. She stared out the restaurant window through smoky eyes, thin fingers turning the cigarette package over and over, as if she were shuffling cards. Marie thought, am I so mean that someone else's trouble feels like a contagious disease? But what can you say?

So Marie let Wanda continue, as her tone descended into shrill sarcasm:

His sister was there, of course. Amanda. She made a slightly better stab at grief, though it's hard when you're fresh in love. Oh yeah, it's still on. This time they made no effort to hide it. He must have thrown his arms around her a dozen times. Poor, poor dear, losing your real mother too, and the one who kept you, did not throw you back. That must be doubly hard.

Then there was the whole saga of the half brother, Hart. Oh I guess I didn't tell you. He's dead too. The Lord giveth and the Lord taketh back, all in the same season. Heart attack, or a stroke, on September 11, no less. Keeled over while he was talking on the phone down in L.A. They rushed him to the hospital, but it was too late. Well, we never got to know Hart. Only saw him once, in that restaurant. I had a feeling that I might have liked him. Maybe that's because he took an instant dislike to Neil, stalked out of the restaurant before his pie, which come to think of it, was right around the same time I began to take a slow, steady dislike to Neil too. You could say it started then.

At this point Wanda stopped talking and began to cry. Dry sobs twisted her gaunt face. Marie wanted to look away though she resisted, and instead, fished a Kleenex out of her purse.

Wanda's love for Neil was flaming red, her hatred, purple. Hot coloured feelings gave her strength. She blew her nose and continued:

No, Neil did not go up there for Hart's funeral. Apparently there wasn't one. I didn't really pay attention. It's nothing to me. Apparently his ashes have been held up at the border for weeks, some problem with his papers. I'll tell you, Marie, this whole thing has brought out another side to Neil. He hardly even speaks to me, and if he does it's to say something so useless I wish he'd keep his mouth shut. When a man like that takes his love away, you're left with nothing but a big, stony heap of silence. He doesn't even pretend! Sometimes, just to test, I'll throw my arms around him and give him a big kiss. He kisses me back for a second and then he points his head over my shoulder and

I can feel he's looking at something behind my back. Anything, just looking somewhere else. I can feel it. He's always saying, we've got to get away together, Wanda, just the two of us. Second honeymoon. But when? Never, that's when. It will never happen. I will never again be alone with my husband. It's all over. Come and gone, Neil and Wanda.

I know what people are saying, that it's me, my fault. I'm having some kind of breakdown. The change of life, all that. Insanity runs in my family. Ha! They're saying Neil's a brick. He is. But I'll tell you why. He's being nice to me so I'll be the one to go and he'll get the kids. I can see right through his strategy. He's a patient man, always has been. And I am not. I'm the sensitive one, the one who gets things done, takes the plunge. That's one of the reasons we were so good together. Opposites attract. But when one of the opposites pulls away . . .

I almost wish I could go like Hart. Quick and on the phone. I wish my ashes were in a box and being held for safe keeping by federal authorities. Maybe I should make a will.

Marie wanted to tell Wanda to trust the Lord, but such advice seemed both obvious and pointless. To get any good out of trusting the Lord, you have to be in a trusting frame of mind, and Wanda clearly was not. Instead, she mentioned someone in their church group who knew a counsellor – at which point Wanda blew up and started using foul language with regards to Neil and Amanda, so Marie did not continue. She lacked the confidence to advise Wanda further, though she herself was in a trusting mood, able to look her friend straight in the eye. By then it was obvious that the next person to hear her troubles would have to be a professional.

"I will pray to the Lord for you," Marie said. "Night and day, for as long as it takes."

Wanda muttered thank you and they parted company. That was the last time Marie saw Wanda Springer.

❧ VI ❧

HART'S NOTEBOOK

I

VANCOUVER. Train headed east. 10/April/02   5:30 p.m.
Mountain Time.

Dollar store notebook, pen in hand, the point being to get
it all down before it goes. Seven months – black hole in an
otherwise cramped life. Last few days still burning. Coffin
lowered into a muddy hole, the obscene waste of my fifty
years gone down too, sucked out by the poor bugger's final
ordeal. Dust to dust, if the rain ever stops. (I would have
opted for cremation, but it was not my funeral.)

   Put R's death on hold for now. Concentrate on what
happened before he died/after I died/the time in between.
Figure out what it means. Above all, foremost in this effort
to record, wherever it leads – HOLD ON TO CERTAINTY.
What happens next has never been so clear – the PURPOSE
OF ALMIGHTY LIVING/contrast with relentless trudge
from one stimulant to the next, otherwise known as the past
= a monumental waste of time. By all means resist the urge

to slide back, lose sight. Risk of forgetting is high. Must hold on to this precious knowledge, hold on for life.

While I scribbled the above, a toad flopped into the seat opposite mine. Stains on his crotch, greasy hair, skunky beard. To ward off conversation, I stared back. He got the message, buried his snout in the *Sun*. Now he's peeking over the page, watching me write this. I pretend not to notice. He stinks. So do I, but for a reason . . . . Still making excuses. Every stink has its raison d'être. In spite of all that's happened, kindness does not come easily. Note to Self: learn to love humanity.

Toad, still watching. Can't do this if he intends to keep on staring. Nothing natural or literary going on here, yet crucial. Must get to the end before the train pulls into Montreal and life starts up again and the last few months die out behind my back. Head down, keep the pen moving. Avoid revision. Hide nothing. Otherwise, these pages will be blanked out/used up /gone by Moose Jaw. Don't even know if we stop in Moose Jaw. Forgot to ask.

Where to start? That's the hard part. The beginning – death/birth.

Lower the lights.

OPENING SCENE: a dimly lit hospital room, night, L.A. Man – middle-aged, white male (played by Kevin Spacey?) wakes up, finds himself in bed, staring at the ceiling. He looks around. Camera pulls back to reveal a lump in the bed next to his, head & body covered with a sheet, bare toes sticking out, pointing at the ceiling.

How did he get there? Distant ambulance siren arouses faint memory. Sound: a crash.

FLASHBACK: the final minutes come back to him in a rush, accompanied by a headache. Chair upended while he was on the phone.

On the other end of the line, a woman, breathing. *Hello, hello?* He calls her name, twice. *Sandrine*. She says nothing. A dog barks.

BLACKOUT

FADE UP ON Night in L.A. Not to be confused with darkness or silence. Merely a slowdown. Neon light through Venetian blinds casts shadow bars across the two hospital beds. Moved by an overwhelming need to piss, man staggers toward a toilet at the end of the room, a pungent cell smelling of cleanser and weakness of the flesh. Catches a frightening sight in the mirror: a thick bandage on the back of his head, sunken eyes. Souvenir of the crash, head hitting the floor. He remembers gripping the phone, ambulance, etc. The rest is vague. Something unpleasant must have happened to trigger the attack. That's the pattern. When it's over, the effort to remember feels like a hangover.

His head hurts. Further sleep being unlikely, he takes up a position on the windowsill and prepares to watch the insomniac city change shift.

Time passes. The man in the other bed stirs, shakes off the sheet revealing thin spikes of hair dyed yellow. A porcupine, breathing hard. Or an old motor full of snorts and gasps. *Hawwchhhhh-hhhchwwaahh.*

Woken by his own roar, the lump sits up Lazarus-like, swings bare legs over the side of the bed. Feet barely touching the floor, gown twisted round his waist, he slumps, belches, raises a leg to fart. A steep staircase of wind, carnivorous swamp gas fallout – bowel talk, a common language.

The lump gropes his way toward the toilet and falls onto the seat, leaving the door open. A lumbering barrel of excrement, thunder, groans, a few choice words.

The man observes, listens, disgusted. Stays as far away from the storm as possible, crouches against the glass wall, gaze fixed on the skyline view. He makes an effort to recall the recent past, a blind girl and a dog. If not for the phone call, a semi-sober fatally blocked screenplay writer would have eaten a meal with a lovely German girl and either gone on to write a phenomenally successful art house road pic, or slept with her, or both. Or neither.

He resolves to dwell not upon the aborted future of the past, instead to dwell happily on the German girl. She was travelling alone, with dog. The phone rang. He got up to answer. Turned his back and saw her feed her steak to the dog, a scene reflected in the plate-glass door. He resolves to find the girl and explain everything:

These attacks happen under stress, nothing serious. A shot of adrenaline helps. Lovely Leni? . . . Lena. Warm thoughts are easy when the subject is a beauty. But reverie is overtaken by a battle royal raging in the toilet. Roars, then singing, more like a chant:

A chi yam Mi kwa mo yich / A chi yam Mi kwa mo yich / A chi yam . . .

Chanting merges with groans and grunts, all part of the same ludicrous ritual, the desperate struggle of shit to escape human captivity. Observer inclined to bolt but he is wearing a hospital gown, bare ass, no shoes. He closes his eyes and waits for time to pass.

A chi yam Mi kwa mo yich / A chi yam Mi kwa mo yich / A chi yam . . .

(In the months that followed, the dying R would bring me back to this scene, to the strange cacophony of excretion. My first careless account based on cursory observations took up residence in his morphine-soaked brain, to be trotted out again and again over the winter. It is entirely possible my recollection has little to do with what actually happened. Embellished by telling, it may by now be nothing but a memory of a memory, the sum of countless times I chanted the chant at R's bedside, danced the dance described by R in minute detail, commanded by R, when he was too weak to show me how. He insisted I follow instructions and dance in his place.

A chi yam Mi kwa mo yich / A chi yam Mi kwa mo yich./ A chi yam . . .)

Finally, the toilet fell quiet. Sleepwalking bear reappeared, clear-eyed, naked, heading in my direction, diminished but content, gutted, drained, wrung out by a bowel storm, better than a jerk off. How I envied his relief! Watched him shuffle past, oblivious, pivot, groan and fall like a hundred-year-old dead elm onto my bed. He lay on his stomach, palms of his hands, bare ass pointed at the ceiling, face squashed against the pillow. A dead man's pose, except that he was still breathing – deep and peaceful. Lips parted, breathing on my pillow. Correction, bleeding on my pillow. A nasty facial wound opened up during the orgy of relief. Bruises exposed and seeping.

I poked at his shoulder.

"Hey, hey, you. Get up. Move on, eh?"

Nothing.

"Wake up!" I slapped him hard on the ass. Noted surprisingly hard buttocks. Not a man who sits for a living. The breathing stopped. A long, still moment, finally, he sucked back a gulp of air and fell back into the rhythm of sleep.

Considered buzzing the nurses' station, rejected that notion as too much trouble and resumed my place at the window. I have never been able to sleep in a room where someone else is sleeping, unless first collapsing under the influence of too much liquor (one of Sandrine's many complaints). Why should the snoring presence of a shit-free fellow male make any difference? But it did.

Giving up on sleep, I elected to pursue my nocturnal consideration of lovely Lena, focus on all that real blonde hair. In a town where everything that moves is some kind of blonde, hers was so real to the roots it seemed phoney. Her dog Gustav had tufts of gold in his mane and intelligent brown eyes, the seeing side of Lena's milky blues. They made an attractive couple. A girl brimming with juicy life and her patient dog, poised for attack. It would be no hardship to stay up all night thinking of Lena.

However, I slept. No memory of getting into the empty bed. Blank. Opened my eyes on daylight, shadows gone. I was stretched out on my back, tucked up like real patient. The bed next to me – my bed – was empty.

What happened next can only be explained by the convergence of external political forces and the deepest eddies of personal destiny. Or, I screwed up as usual by jumping on an impulse.

The door opened and an attractive woman entered followed by an obviously younger man, both wearing white lab coats, tension between them. Conversation in progress seemed to revolve around a disagreement concerning the female doctor's husband, something he had said or done or found out, which bore upon the younger doctor's plans for the weekend. Once or twice they referred to each other as doctor, in italics. Disagreement seemed to veer between the task at hand and recreation, medical terminology flung about, staccato pace, all of it dripping in sticky innuendo, the familiar fallout of intimacy. They had not come into the room exclusively out of concern for me. I feigned sleep.

Professional attention focused on the chart at the foot of my bed. She took my pulse, listened to my chest, scribbled a few words, then having ascertained I was still alive, her interest flagged. He concentrated exclusively on a series of plaintive and futile (so easy to judge from a distance) gestures. Pressure mounted until, out of the corner of my eye, I noticed her hold up one finger and the argument stopped. Sensing this sudden need for silence had something to do with me, my living presence, I took no more risks, kept my eyes shut, jaw slack like a deep-sleeping idiot. Sounds of shuffling at the foot of the bed, a pen scratching on the clipboard, then they left the room.

I wandered into the toilet. The floor was littered with scraps of bandage, shredded toilet paper, a soiled nightgown in tatters – the dead man's last hurrah, old skin discarded in the struggle to escape. His presence filled the tiny room. Life after death? Highly unlikely, but this man left a powerful aura. I reached down, picked up a plastic wristband he'd ripped off in the fracas. In the place of a name was a series of strange words, *Okanch amamoweech nda ndouie*. (Meaning, I would learn later, Animals Gathering Together in the Wilds. Poetry. At first glance, hardly befitting the ranter who ruined my sleep and bled on my pillow, yet weeks later, once I learned what the name meant, why he had thrown off his given name and taken another, I saw it fit perfectly. In due time, this blurry night would grow into something else.)

At the foot of his bed – where I'd slept – was a chart bearing the poetic name. Also on the chart, in a bold affirmative hand, the lady doctor had scrawled: TO BE DISCHARGED. My bed had been stripped, my chart was gone.

It took a few seconds to get the picture. The stranger was dead. His identity, however, was alive and well and beckoning. By contrast, I was officially 'dead.'

I was seized by a fierce desire to leave the premises.

Had I thought it through, I would have dismissed the idea as implausible. Ridiculous. But I didn't think. Mischief or a deep-seated need to bolt or both led me to a cupboard tucked behind the door, where I found his clothing: tattered jeans, stained t-shirt, pointy-toed crooner boots and a rusty buckskin jacket with fringes up the arms. I put it on. Everything fit. Felt like a costume, which gave me a boost. I tucked the dead man's chart under my arm and headed for the door.

There was no one around at the nurse's station, the hall was deserted too, as if a bomb scare had emptied the place and left me behind. (Which as it turned out was not far from the truth.) Finally I found them, patients and staff crowded around a TV set in the lounge, watching what many mistook that day for a third-rate disaster movie. An airplane diving into a tower, flames, smoke. Then another one.

At the admitting desk, a clerk took a look at the chart, and after consulting with someone in authority who hardly took her eyes off the TV screen, fetched a plastic bag and filled it with the dead man's valuables – battered shoulder bag, a medallion on a leather string. Thus I walked out of the building into a blazing day, September 11, 2001, high as a kite. A man about to fool the world, floating on a buzz of certainty. Oh rare state: delusion and conviction. I was eager to embrace both.

LATER. Four stops before midnight and we aren't even out of B.C. This train is a milk run. Might have known. The self-appointed spy occupying the seat across from mine has wandered off, meaning I am free to recline at ease and put my feet up, at least until the conductor comes by. Beginning to regret not booking a bunk. Too expensive but this posture is excruciating. Handwriting, a mess, jerky scrawl, impossible to read. Should leave off till I get back to Montreal and buy a laptop, rent a hotel room, take time. But time risks contamination. So, press on like a train slogging through the mountains & get it all down. My wrist burns.

I returned to the beach house briefly. Found the spare key under the flowerpot and entered, careful to stay away from windows. Eerie sensation – felt like I was intruding on someone else's life. The laptop and pile of notes seemed to mock. Saw in an instant how foolish I'd been to think I could escape into movieland – plumb an empty well and thereby start again? Not likely. I'd simply dragged the worst of Self to another location. Pocketed $1950 U.S., paused over the palm pilot (hitherto my most valuable possession), decided to leave it behind. At the last minute, grabbed up a couple of credit cards.

During the still-light hours of a day the media-crazed world now knows as 9/11, I strolled the empty streets of Los Angeles in a daze. Sirens in the distance, people huddled around any and all TVs, police and firemen everywhere. Somehow footage of mass murder/suicide did not register. It was distant, fictional, I being obsessed by the death of a stranger who checked out in my sleeping presence.

How could a guy who made so much noise taking a shit die so quietly? When did I fall asleep? I had no memory of getting into his bed. Blackout? Denial? *I slept through a man's death.* That part irked. For months after that, a black mood would dominate my existence. Deep, thick remorse, like I'd done something, but what? Nothing leaped out. Looked at rationally, nothing could explain the cloud of dread. For now I felt guilty of something clear and awful: sleeping through a man's death. Makes no logical sense. Had I not slept, he would still be dead. But for some reason, I sensed that I definitely WAS somehow implicated. It was not good.

(Months later, when I was forced to recall that night ad nauseam, I started dreaming I'd actually tried to get into bed with him but he wouldn't let me do it. In another dream, we were jammed into the same coffin, one of us dead, the other not, it kept changing. Typical sexual-panic nightmares inspired by a fairly bizarre slice of reality? Time out of Self? As if something in me died with him. I did not know who or what to mourn. That's it. It's coming clearer. More later.)

NIGHT TRAIN. The overhead lights just went out. Like boarding school, all passengers must obey. Some are slumped into balls, some moaning, drunk, others flopped out on the floor. I am pulled down into this backbreaking seat by a deep need to sleep. (Maybe that's how it happened. I was tired, I fell asleep, he died. Still, the sleeping bit caught me off guard.)

I drift. I drift. I always do.

DAWN. We're into the Rockies. I'm stiff in tender places. Ate a couple of doughnuts from hastily packed rations. Train food is hideously expensive. No sign of Toad. He must have found a bunk. Hope he stays there. Cloudless sky. Spectacular vista, duly seen and noted. Must take instruction from the slow train east – stay on the rails.

So: another man's shoes. After a lengthy existential wander, I went into a diner for a cup of coffee, my intention being to make a rigorous search of every scrap of the deceased's paperwork in order to form an idea of just who I was about to become. Precious little to go on, still, I believed this particular exchange had happened for a reason. At the time, I was fully aware of SOMETHING HAPPENING, charged atmosphere, mind open to the vagaries of chance. Things happened leading up to L.A. that put me in the mood to bolt. L.A. was obviously not far enough. Leave it at that for now.

I rummaged through his shoulder bag, found a few crumpled receipts, a half-dozen individually wrapped mint-flavoured toothpicks, return part of a bus ticket from Vancouver plus $18 and change. Identification consisted of a laminated red and beige photo ID card declaring the owner to be a bona fide Status Indian and member of the Cree Nation of Great Whale, Quebec. Family name, Meadows, but he

went by the name of *Okanch amamoweech nda ndouie.*
Strange, though it matched the one on his hospital wristband. He looked old beyond his years, dyed hair thinning.
Yes, in a pinch the blurry photo could be me. But the rest
of his identity would not be easy to fake. In fact, impossible. I knew there was no chance I could pass myself off as a
'native person.' No offence implied. On the contrary, I'm
sure the angry tribes would agree. I, Hart Granger, would
make a hell of an odd red man. A bum or an immigrant,
maybe. I do accents. But the Sacred Founding People, I con-
cluded right away, are off limits. Out of my league. I do not
identify. I could not drown myself in him.

The sudden loss of a great plan sent me plunging straight
back into the black mood, which is when I realised how
good it had felt to imagine escape. From? Self, what else. I
was sick to death of My Self, knew every corner of Self's
faults, weaknesses, old tricks. Was royally bored by Self's scams
and delusions. Unconvinced that life is worth the effort. Suici-
dal? Nothing that glamorous, just sick of it all.

By the third coffee, darkness had closed in. What now?
I had no idea.

The waitress brought over the bill. Without thinking, I
reached into the inside jacket pocket for my wallet. My wallet?
Not even my pocket. Came out with a wad of papers. Letters,
still in the envelopes but worn and bent around the edges, like
they'd been sat on for years, and addressed to the dead man.
A feminine script, big flowery strokes, long, thin letters, t's
crossed with a squiggle and i's dotted by circles. Real ink.
Almost childlike, definitely a woman's handwriting.

News that the now-breathless farter had had a woman in
his life perked me up considerably, a testimony no doubt to

the shallowness of my despair. I ripped open the first letter and began to read. 'To my dearest brother . . .' Long, gushy, rambling thoughts. I cringed but could not stop reading.

The dates stretched back several months. A single theme permeated every page: she wanted him to come home. The dead man's sister had a simple, direct way of expressing her concern, totally in keeping with the childishness of the script. I imagined her about fifteen, at least what you would imagine a fifteen-year-old girl to be like if you didn't actually know one. She wrote vaguely about her life, interspersing a few personal scraps with pleas for news of the recipient's happiness, health, plans for return.

The most encouraging passage and also the most heart-rending came in the final letter, dated late summer. If the wayward brother chose to persist in his silence, he should know that she would be waiting in a certain Vancouver café every Friday afternoon at five p.m., sitting over a cup of coffee, expecting him to walk in. This schedule she vowed to keep 'for the rest of my natural life.'

Signed: Waiting Forever, R – scrawl, upward. I thought it said 'Renée.' I thought I understood.

An image of the letter writer quickly took shape, a dark-haired waif (variation on the German girl?) Surely an innocent.

Whereas I was a thief.

By stealing a dead man's identity, I had ensured she would never know what happened to her brother. Living with false hope, she would inevitably grow hard and bitter. Although the letters had not been written to me, I was all the letter-writer had left, the thread that linked her to the truth. Thus the void left by the melt down of my impersonation fantasy

began to fill up with a mission: I must find Renée, bring her
the news of his death, provide at least the consolation of
knowing her brother was no longer wandering alone in the
vast wasteland of America. That he had died, and with –
well – a certain amount of dignity. At least he had died in bed.

(NOTE: the initial sizzle of an unknown female presence soon gave way to noble sentiments of consolation, compassion – all entirely appropriate feelings in the case of a
deceased's sister. Although admittedly, my dreams at the time
did confuse Renée with Lena. Ghost-like figures languished
in a suspended state of unknowing, me trying to speak, but
no words coming out.)

The full story would need careful consideration. A grieving family member might well blame the witness, or at least
question his version of events. Certainly nothing should be
said to suggest that the bearer of bad news was in any way
personally implicated. How soon the scheming mind for-
gets unnecessary edges. I was, even then, as always, covering my butt.

Problem: unless I went back to the beach house and
changed, I would be wearing the deceased's clothes. I saw
myself returning to the scene, packing a small overnight bag.
The telephone rings. It will be Sandrine, wondering about her
visit, the fatal phone call. I pictured letting it ring and ring and
ring, walking out on the ringing phone, leaving the beach
house forever. Let her wonder whatever happened to Hart.
Thus I decided not to go back for a change of clothes. I could
not walk away from my life with a telephone ringing.

Gathering up the letters, which were now my sworn duty
to deliver, I recalled seeing a return bus ticket to Vancouver.
Miraculously, it had not yet expired. Surely an omen. (Around

this time, omens and coincidences began to play a major part in my day-to-day decisions. I looked for external guidance before taking the smallest step. I could not order a cheeseburger unless something happened to direct my choice, which is why eventually even the need to eat became too troublesome. I'd put it off as long as possible . . . Later, later.)

I paid for the coffee and walked out into daylight in search of the bus station. An hour later I was on my way north, filled with the best of intentions. Bearing the healing elixir of news from a long lost beloved brother, albeit bad news.

Endless agonizing ride through the night, into September 12 (actual beginning of a new century?). At the border, all passengers were hauled off the bus. I was searched and tossed into jail, alongside a handful of other adult males whose main cause for suspicion was a swarthy appearance. Only one Arab among us, and he was travelling with his pregnant wife, whose face was veiled. She was searched but not detained. Worse: they locked him up and sent her away, alone.

These details I recall, but at the time I was amazed to find the border guards actually took me for a native person. Believed my false ID! I did my best to play along. Rattled the iron bars and shouted, "You can't do this me. I'll sue your balls off! My whole tribe will sue!!!"

The guards looked at me strangely, as did a (true) native son in the cell next to mine. Apparently members of the First Nations do not normally threaten litigation from a jail cell. Anyway, it didn't work. So I flashed the letters, told them I had to go home to inform my sister of a death in the family. Faced with commonplace familial matters, they seemed to lose interest, and at dawn, let me go – an experience confirming the power of lies which contain a smattering of truth.

At least, conviction. In the absence of truth, conviction will suffice.

For the first time in years, I was filled with conviction. Purpose. I was certain that finding Renée was necessary and somehow important, not just another appointment trumped up by an impostor whose job it was to keep the material world spinning.

II

Vancouver was an unknown city to me, hitherto irrelevant. Apart from a few blurry business trips, I'd spent no time there. Suddenly it was the centre of the universe: Terminal and Main Streets. Omens everywhere.

The bus pulled in shortly after 10 p.m. I took a cab uptown to the Hampton Hotel on Robson Street. Altercation at check-in over my insistence on paying cash: sorry "Sir," no corporate rate without ID (and, she should have added, appropriate attire). Finally I was ensconced in a hot bath with a mug of cold beer, soon dove straight for the bed and much-needed sleep. Woke up at 1 a.m., rested, impatient. Wandered downstairs to look for the bar.

Retracing my steps over those first few days, what hits me now is the ungodly amount of money I haemorrhaged in the pursuit of nothing more important than comfort and killing time – didn't give it a second thought! Lived those first few days as if on expenses for Harvin Investments Inc., turning grumpy if every twitch of appetite was not instantly sated. How the Mighty Have Fallen. What I spent in three days would have kept me for a month. Present menu: a duffle bag crammed with cheap tinned meat and doughnuts, enough to last till Montreal. I eat now only to quell hunger.

The next morning I resolved to familiarise myself with the environment in which the news would be delivered. I started by locating our rendezvous point – the Ovaltine Café, 251 East Hastings. Neon beacon, like some kind of fifties movie set (think Wim Wenders). A real diner with chrome stools and a bar, over-varnished wood, Formica tables, leatherette booths and mirrors everywhere, all of it soaked in a ripe marinade of grease. Not the ambiance I had imagined. The fantasy sister was firmly lodged in my mind's eye: she would be cute and she would stay cute even through tears. No, the Ovaltine would not be a suitable backdrop for my performance as a sensitive stranger. Of this I was certain.

I slipped into a booth ($3 minimum per person). Sipping watery coffee, I studied the patrons (a ropey lot) and glanced at a newspaper. Loud headlines, shock and horror. Photos of people holding hands or solo, jumping to their death from the flaming towers of the World Trade Centre. Agony, anguish. I stared at the pictures. Catastrophe was shaking up the world that day and yet all I could think about was finding a stranger who might or might not be lost. (Was there a connection? I'm tempted now to find one, but that would be bullshit. At the time, none of it seemed real, or important.)

No, I was preoccupied with the details of how and where this other revelation would take place. On my way back to the hotel, I made a thorough study of the bistros and cafés of Gastown. My priorities were soft lighting and privacy. I considered the Cannery, but feared ostentation, settled finally on a leafy, seafood place with skylights called Inventions, partly for the name, but also for its atmosphere of solace.

Back at the hotel, I flaked out in front of the TV until it was time for bed. Woke up at dawn – Friday – with an advanced case of nerves. Uncharacteristic, to say the least. The last time I'd stayed at the Hampton, the future of our near-total bluff of a money management firm hung on my ability to talk a room full of corporate stiffs into abandoning the safe status quo and entrusting their capital to Hart & Vincent (Harvin Investments). I spilled not one drop of sweat over that venture and we succeeded marvellously, although I recall dear Vince did some sweating.

Now, I was about to meet a stranger, give her news of someone I'd never officially met. No personal stake whatsoever, yet I was terrified. Also deeply excited. A virgin schoolboy full of hope. Not that I thought – no, no, no. My fantasies were not of a carnal nature. Tingle in the gut, no lower. I was able to visualise her down to the sweeping eyelashes and she was beautiful, but also (according to the full-blown extravaganza of my dreams that night) something of an angel. My fantasies went no farther than the sight of her melting, me reaching out. Fade to dark, darker blue then black.

By early afternoon I'd had four cups of coffee (at various uptown bistros which far exceeded the Ovaltine's minimum). Was much too keyed up to keep wandering around town until five, so I went back to the hotel room, intending to dial up a movie. Fell instantly into a deep sleep. Woke up at six.

Six p.m.!!!! It was pouring rain.

I tore down to the Ovaltine in a cab. The manager recognised me from several preparatory coffees. He swore he had no memory of the lady I was expecting to meet, and knew of no young woman who'd been coming in every Friday at five p.m. When I pressed him, he shouted, "NO!" and told me to get out. Only later did I realise he must have been put on guard by rumours of dozens of prostitutes mysteriously gone missing, and the mounting suspicion of a serial killer stalking the neighbourhood. Did I look that rough? I did. Desperate? I was.

Paralysed by disappointment, I veered out into the street, stood in the rain, thinking uncharitable thoughts about the low-life characters shuffling across my retina. Knew I was falling into the familiar pit of self-loathing and anger that lurks at the bottom of all my frustrations. Overcome by a familiar want of spiritual calm, I was getting ready to kick something or somebody. Tempted to hail a cab and head for the airport.

What to do? Wait an entire week for a meeting that would probably come down to an awkward ten minutes? The balloons of fantasy prick easily. The idea of more waiting made me frantic. One whole week alone, nothing to do. Too much for a man who had never of his own free will taken a day's vacation, rarely spent a (sober) evening home alone . . .

Nevertheless, I resolved to wait.

The first thing I did was move to the Afton Hotel, a seedy establishment right next to the Ovaltine. Ironic altercation with management. Was I too well dressed for this place? They made me pay the week in advance.

Putting in time was as bad as I'd expected. Spent several afternoons at the library, Safdie's odd cake of a building modelled on the Coliseum, trying to find out more about R's family background, tribe, anything that might be useful in establishing contact. The library had an impressive collection of books on the Cree, ranging from exotic picture books to furious tomes on how the northern peoples had been ripped off by 'progress.' As was my habitual approach to facing complex subjects on a tight deadline, I skimmed, taking careful note of a few precise pieces of information that might be dropped into conversation. For example, that they call themselves the Eeyouch and they live in Eeyou Istchee – the People's land, and they've been there for the past 5000 years.

The family name was Meadows. At first I assumed it was a typical native name, but my research revealed it to be ancient Orkney. The Meadows were descendents of Scottish fiddlers who'd come over from the Orkney Islands in the early 1700s to work for the Hudson's Bay Company. According to what I read, this explains the appearance of a few red-haired babies. It also accounts for the lively fiddling tradition, and a discernable penchant for the drinking of tea. The man whose identity I'd stolen definitely did not have red hair. Inevitably, though, my image of his sister shifted once more, to include genteel Celtic maidenhood.

It was a very long week, immensely boring but worthwhile, in retrospect. What I thought of then as "putting in time" would eventually become my way of life. Withdrawal from meaningful/meaningless activity is surprisingly difficult. Excruciating loneliness mixed with idleness is a mind-crushing combination. It is a sobering and finally enlightening experience to face a succession of completely blank days. Appreciation sets in slowly. Given the void, my mission loomed large.

I re-read the letters, practically memorised them, studied the curly scrawl that lifted optimistically toward the top right side of the page.

Finally, Friday arrived. I parked myself at the Ovaltine shortly after four, determined not to miss her again. Took a seat at a table facing the door. The staff recognised me. I sensed they were on full alert, nods and eye contact all around. Five o'clock came and went. I flipped through the newspapers, worked at staying calm.

By 5:45 I decided she wasn't going to show. What to do? Leave a note and head for the airport? By six, I'd begun to get my mind around the idea of putting in another week, because maybe something had happened. She could have been tied up. After all, she'd been keeping up the vigil for more than a year, so it was not unreasonable that from time to time life might intervene. While I was formulating excuses, a slim figure of youth walked through the door, stopped and looked around.

I knew immediately, it was her. Back lit by light from the street, face obscured, a lanky frame. Fine features hiding behind long dark hair. Shoulders slightly stooped, a body in a hurry to get going, not at all comfortable on the planet. She scanned the room, lowered her head a little further, then turned to go.

I got up and followed her out the door. Tapped her on the shoulder.

"Excuse me, are you looking for . . . ?" I took a deep breath, and spit out the dead man's poetic name. It startled her. Then I noticed – she was a he.

"René?" As the word left my mouth, I must have blushed blood red, disappointment falling like a hammer. I went limp, held up only by the gaze of fierce brown eyes radiant with suspicion.

He nodded. "You know my brother?"

"I did," I said, solemnly.

And that was it, bad news delivered on the street like a punch in the gut. He turned away, and I thought, he's going to cry. But he just stood there, rigid.

"I'm terribly sorry," I stammered. "Really, I've come up from L.A. to tell you. He gave me your letters in the event of . . ."

On and on I went, a string of half-truths – make that lies – each one setting me up for hours of further fabrication. But standing in the gloom of East Hastings at eventide, I figured I needed to invent the missing details, embellish a brief implausible encounter between the dead brother and me, give the survivor what he needed to take in this terrible truth. And I admit, babbling was also a way to dig myself out of the face-numbing void created by the collapse of a powerful fantasy.

So I would not get to console a grief-stricken beauteous sister? Instead, I offered to buy a stiff-jawed native Indian pup a coffee. His eyes brimmed with what at that exact moment looked a lot like rage. His hair had a reddish hue, and I thought, don't tell me you play the fiddle?

He said nothing, just turned and went back into the Ovaltine. I followed. The waiter shouted something at him that I didn't catch, and he raised an arm in a salute. So they were on friendly terms. I just hadn't asked the right questions.

We slid into a booth. Noticing him glance up at a plate of food going by, I suggested he might like something to eat. Without consulting the menu, he ordered a hearty meal. As he ate, he kept glancing at himself in the mirror by our table, face frozen in the kind of expression an innocent third party might have mistaken for annoyance.

I wasn't particularly hungry, but ordered a club sandwich to be polite. Luckily so, because the first hour we spent together was excruciating, great yawning gaps between my pathetic attempts at conversation and his minimalist replies. In my newly tenderised state, this was almost worse than solitude. Finally I gave up, just sat back and worked on the food. Once I'd stopped trying to manufacture conversation, silence purified the air and he started to talk.

He didn't seem surprised to hear I knew his family was Cree, from Northern Quebec. Still, finding out we hailed from the same province didn't exactly cause him to bloat up with feelings of kinship. Finally he broached the subject of his brother. Did he suffer? I tried not to go too far beyond the actual facts, such as they were. Let's just say he inferred a great deal from a few thin comments. He decided I'd known his brother well, and after that, nothing I said seemed to change his mind. Now he wanted the full picture of his life and death. I scrambled for a way out, finally hit upon a solution: during the time we'd known each other, I said, I had respected his privacy and not asked too many questions. But (yes, all right, this I invented) his brother's last thoughts had definitely been homeward. He surely had been on his way home. Witness the return bus ticket, which I had been able to put to use.

His face remained impassive while we talked. He rubbed his eye at one point as if to clear away a tear, but maybe not. I had no idea what he was thinking. No clue as to what he thought of me. But it mattered. I wasn't exactly expecting gratitude. Well, maybe I was. At least acknowledgement, some sign of my existence.

When we finished our refills of coffee, he said he had to be going, thanked me for supper. Pocketing the receipt, I said, don't mention it, I'm up here on business. A flicker of amusement passed across his rock hard eyes, as if to say, what business could this possibly be? Maybe I was paranoid. In a place like the Downtown Eastside, a dude dressed in snake boots and oily buckskin would fit right into the only business that ever gets done. I willed my face into a shifty smirk and shrugged, hoping he'd be satisfied with innuendo. Let him think I'm a drug lord, what did it matter? He waited till I moved first, then hurried off in the opposite direction, and for all I knew, that was the end of it.

To say the meeting was a letdown would be an understatement. I was numb. Empty. A state of extreme sobriety.

I still had some cash left and no real desire to be anywhere else. Decided not to contact anyone back in Montreal or give signs of my whereabouts, meaning no using the credit cards. (A resolution I've kept, with some difficulty.) The past, Sandrine, my newly bloated family, Vince and his machinations – all of it left me monumentally indifferent. They'd find out soon enough the dead body was not that of Hart Granger, and then what? I hardly cared. I decided to embrace being dead, to enjoy it while it lasted.

October – glorious weather. My little cell of a room provided refuge after hours of walking. Once I had nothing to wait for, no anticipation, time ceased to drag. I hung limp, ready to be carried by a self-generated wind. Putting in a day came down to resisting going back to Montreal, which turned out to be very, very easy.

The neighbourhood of my orbit was the Downtown Eastside, a Mecca for both the drug world and a certain youthful, terminally trendy smart set, though in my estimation, the latter is losing the turf war. It's an anthill of activity, hundreds of human drones hauling huge crumbs across enormous distances, all of it squeaky essential and oh-so-futile. I drifted, soaking up people, street life, taking in the plethora of faces – worn down, pumped up, sometimes grotesque and eventually, familiar. So many schemes, deals, ruses, heartbreaks, scams, crimes, encounters, business-sexual-drug deals. Not being part of it, I was able to take a good, hard look.

This is Life.

Watching human existence thunder on without my participation put me in a philosophical mood. I started to think around and over (if not exactly through) the main events in my life, the key decisions and pivotal moments, and this thinking turned my breath foul. Each day loomed like a shrinking block of solid time. I ate less, spent less, walked and walked and walked. Whole days went by when I did not hear the sound of my own voice. Seemed like months, though it was actually somewhere around ten days.

Then one evening I ran into him on the street. He was not looking well, though when he saw me, he did a kind of double take, as if he'd passed a mirror.

"Hello!" I said.

He stopped walking. "You're still here?"

An awkward exchange, it carried us straight into the nearest bar. The thought flashed through my frog-belly-liberal mind that offering to buy an Indian booze was not exactly a kind idea, but it was too late. Anyway, he ordered a cranberry juice so I took one too. His face seemed to have collapsed.

Hollow cheeks, thousands of pockmarks, parched lips. I had remembered clear, sallow skin. At our first encounter, I'd been unnerved by the strong feminine vibration he gave off: high cheekbones, some kind of makeup on his eyes, mascara and eyeliner, if memory serves. I remembered his long, dark-reddish hair was wavy and framed his face. Now it was greasy and tied back in a tight knot. He was gaunt. He looked ill. And, strangely, he was glad to see me, as if we actually knew each other.

"You've lost weight," he said, echoing my observation of him. "You okay?"

"Sure. I've been walking a lot, that's all. Feels good to melt off a few pounds."

"How's business?"

"Business is good. I should be able to leave soon. All depends."

He said he was surprised no one had contacted him about the body. Body? For an instant, I had to run the word through my mind. Yes, yes, the body of his brother. But that would be me! I mean . . . Habeas corpus, naturally, he would want a body.

"That's odd," I said, "I'll look into it when I get back to L.A." I hoped that would be enough.

"I might go down there myself," he said. Then he coughed, great hacking gags that seemed to shake his twig-like frame.

"What's the matter?"

"Nothing," he barked, launching into a second, more unsettling round. In the pale sigh that followed, I could see he definitely wasn't well, but there was nothing to be gained from prying. So I decided to ignore the obvious, and work on conversation. I asked what had brought him to Vancouver in the first place, and he said art. I was about to ask, "Art who?" when the penny dropped.

"Ah. You paint?"

He nodded. "Carve, paint, assemble. Installations. You've heard him play?"

What? It took me an instant to realise he was referring to his late brother. It would be that way for months. In the middle of a quiet moment, he'd make a comment with no introductory clue, as if he was always thinking of his brother. Which is how we fell into the dance. He'd ask a question, I felt compelled to find an answer, as if his silence was a test. So much of what I said came out of a weird compulsion to fill the void. He sucked information out of me. Not all of it true. And some of what was true, I'd rather have kept to myself.

"No, actually, I never heard him play," I sighed, as if I deeply regretted this, implying however that I knew all about the musical side of his multi-faceted personality.

R's face clouded. He looked at me suspiciously.

"Say, what happened to his fiddle?"

"He sold it, I believe." So far, not a single mention of the fact that I was wearing the deceased's coat and boots, which is why I didn't want to leave room for misunderstanding around a musical instrument, in case he blamed me.

Mention of the fiddle seemed to unlock something in him. That's how I came to learn one version of the fraternal success story:

Talent was the brothers' ticket out of a rock-poor northern village even farther north than Great Whale, and a sad family of alcoholics. René took up drawing and carving before he started grade school. A friendly art teacher steered him through the paperwork to finish high school by correspondence, followed by a scholarship to the Emily Carr art school, which brought him to Vancouver.

The first year alone in the big city was gut-wrenching-awful. He was lonely and hard up, about to drop out, when his brother turned up, unrolled his sleeping bag on the kitchen floor and proceeded to launch himself as the next big thing in traditional Celtic fiddle music, with a native twist and an exotic new name. According to René, Vancouver went instantly gaga over the new Ashley MacIsaac. I wasn't at the time following West Coast talent, so I have no idea whether the success he described was as great or as smooth as the telling. Anyway, it paid their bills; René finished art school and almost immediately started selling his stuff. In the space of a few years, both brothers surpassed their humble expectations and entered a lively circle of ambitious young talents on the make.

But as René started winning prizes and selling his works to the rich and guilty (white) corporate types, the musical prodigy went a little mad. Vertigo. He freaked out, headed south, and during the next three years, was heard from intermittently, then not at all. René had a feeling his brother was in serious trouble but he'd never had both the time and money to go down and search for him. Then I turned up and confirmed the worst.

Of course the story had gaps. What could you expect from the duration of one eight-ounce glass of cranberry juice? I had questions, but it took him so long to relate even the bare outline that I didn't dare interrupt. The end came arbitrarily with another fit of coughing, so bad I thought he'd collapse. Telling the story made it worse. He was angry.

"I could sure use the son-of-a bitch now," he said. "Just like him to go and die on me, at a time like this."

"What do you mean?" I said, tempting the mood.

He looked at me for a long, empty minute, but didn't answer. I offered to order some food. He said no, he just needed sleep. So we got up and without discussion headed off. I should say he got up and left. I still don't know what came over me. Maybe the lingering fantasy of a grief-stricken girl tainted my judgement. Or, the real, live surviving brother started to incarnate, fulfil, ooze the creature I'd imagined meeting when I read the curly handwriting soaring off the page like optimistic birds. The two of them blended, filling me with . . . a warm-milk feeling. Compassion? It wasn't a static state. There was something I had to have, or know.

NOTE: looked at from a certain angle, R was all male. But now so thin and sickly, he also put out a girlish side. His beauty was exquisite, beyond gender. Nothing hard or phoney like transvestites on the Main. No, a truly feminine look. Am I nuts? I'm a raving heterosexual. But this guy was confused. Or maybe I mean confusing. Well. He definitely had no problem with his looks. Or with me.

Who knows? About then, clear thinking ended. I followed him like a dog.

His abode was a few blocks away in Gastown, a neighbourhood of galleries, boutiques, bars; a strange mixture of upscale bohemia and drug-scene hubbub. A third-storey loft, it had high ceilings, a wall of windows, glossy hardwood floors and was completely lacking in the normal clutter of home life. The furnishings consisted of a piano, a few large, bold paintings, oddball sculptures and a mattress on the floor.

While I stood gaping, he took a bottle of whiskey out of the cupboard, washed two glasses from a sink full of dirty dishes. When he opened the fridge to get ice, I saw it was empty. He handed me a drink, indicated I should sit on the mattress, and as soon as I did, plopped down beside me. He must have noticed my discomfort. He got up, took a pillow and sat cross-legged, leaning against the wall. We started drinking. Suffice to say he showed remarkable restraint with the whiskey, whereas I did not. This time he did the talking.

As far as I can recall now, he retold the story he'd told in the bar, except that the second time through he did not leave out the hurdles the brothers had crossed to get to the success they so feverishly desired, the asses they'd had to kiss, the appendages they'd had to suck. In the coolest and most unsentimental terms, he laid out the terms of success in the big city.

Far from being naïve, the boys were fiercely ambitious and therefore vulnerable to the whims of movers and shakers in the art world. They soon became playthings for a powerful gallery owner and his friends and colleagues from the international scene. In return, they got the support they needed to launch their careers. Only when René tried to move away from the scene, did he realise what kind of a bargain they'd made.

The end came suddenly. When he started declining his patron's advances, he was cut off. It wasn't just a question of losing support, the guy actually went after René's career, turned his agent against him and started circulating ugly rumours. The scene was small – few players were ready to offend the patron, who had his fingers in many pies. Mixed up in the anguish over his brother's disappearance was the fear that something bad had happened, as punishment for their attempt to break free of the sex circle.

It was a bleak story that made village life in a northern native community look good, even though "traditional" Cree life is no picnic either, straddling the crack between two cultures, one ancient and hard, the other capitalist and spiky. As he talked, René seemed homesick to the point of fever for the open spaces, hunting, fishing, family, the sanity of the known. Yet he swore he would never return, even for a visit, ever. Though he missed it so much it hurt. This puzzled me, but he would not explain.

Thus I got my first big glimpse into the tragically, rigidly divided soul of Native Mankind. I can't speak of course about the entire population. I only know two of them and the late lamented brother was invented along the way. R was a truly messed up individual. As are many people, but this man/boy was unique. I didn't judge, I observed. I thought, you poor son-of-a-bitch. Either your life is over or your life is just beginning. That's the tragedy. Condemned to go on, go to the end, the bottom or top, both look the same. A huge price has been paid to get this far. Out of all that pain, greatness must flow. But you've got to hang on. Hang on.

Can't remember when I've spent that much time listening to somebody's life story. Normally it's What Do You Do? Who Do You Know? Then straight into the present. Hearing him talk was like a movie, one of those searing foreign films, except I was in it. And I felt myself turning into some kind of a cheerleader. Urging him to hang on, don't give up. Pathetic. What else? I had to say something. He was talking to *me*.

The next morning, I woke up deeply hung over, curled tight. My body opened with difficulty, like a stiff fist. R was sprawled out on the hardwood floor, snoring. I stretched my legs, began to pad around the loft, desperate for coffee, but it was not to be had.

In daylight, the art works dominated the room. Huge, colourful scenes, bordering on naïve. Acrylic on canvas, a few on wood. Incredibly precise, as if they should have been miniatures but somehow kept growing. Native motifs, animals, humans, cold coloured landscapes. Social commentaries and pure dynamic images. Almost cartoons, but exquisitely detailed. Emily Carr meets wanker teenage mutant, with attitude. The more I looked at the art, the more I saw René – visual echoes of the way he talked and moved. As if his physical, mental essence – a vapour – had been distilled into liquid and used to make pictures. Eerie.

Slowly, my head cleared. He was still sleeping.

Time to go.

I couldn't find a pen to leave a note, and didn't want to wander off without a word. So I went out and got a couple of tall lattes and a bag of muffins. When I came back he was awake, sitting up on the mattress, shivering. His hands shook when he took the coffee. It spilled over his shirt but he didn't seem to notice. So I stayed, because I couldn't find a pen to leave a note. At least that's what I told myself at the time.

III

PRAIRIES. Passed the last hour in a trance, staring out the window at the sweeping natural effect of sunrise on endless prairie, hundreds of miles of horizon. Bit of a cliché but I've never personally seen anything like this so am in awe – Awe Struck, mesmerised by the stunning visual equivalent of utter boredom, and by that I do not intend to disparage. Takes time to acquire an appreciation for idle empty time, a place where reverie takes root. (By contrast, the Mighty Rockies slid by like an Imax film. I was furiously scribbling and hardly noticed.) This ocean of stubble seems real, seriously tempting. Flashes of what lies ahead . . . Montreal, et al., going back . . . dark. I am tempted to get off in Winnipeg, carry on being dead. Enthusiasm running low. What happened to certainty? Infinite prairie sucks up air. Belly fire flickers. This is harder than I thought. Living again in the early days of R takes me right back . . . Seems like years ago now. I was somebody else then.

R claimed the shakes were a normal part of overwork and stress, a side effect of months spent preparing for an exhibition in New Mexico that had been postponed until next year, totally wearing him out. My first thought was bullshit. This is about your brother. You took the bad news too easily. Of course he wouldn't break down in front of a complete stranger, but eventually grief takes its toll. I decided to stay around a day or two to see him through the bad patch. I went out and bought an air mattress, a sleeping bag and a few groceries. A plant . . . yes, I spent twenty bucks on a flowering plant!

Days went by, he couldn't seem to shake the fatigue. He hardly ate. I spent a lot of time trying to get bits of food into him. I looked at his paintings, tried to get him talking, but he said he wasn't going to paint any more. Didn't want to hear anything about it. Once or twice he sat down at the piano and played a few bars, mostly jazz or a bit of Chopin. Sad memories. He soon gave up.

Apart from my dramatic eyewitness report (which grew with repeated telling), no official word had come to him about his brother's death. He never brought up the body again. I told him the planet is too crowded to eat up all the dead, so the only moral solution is cremation. He didn't agree (as I found out later) but said nothing. I promised as soon as he felt better I would have the ashes delivered and he could scatter them or bury them or whatever, which I still intend to do.

He left it up to me to take charge of practical matters, which I quickly gathered had never been his strong point (understatement of the new century). In many ways R really was the hysterical young girl of the letters: starry-eyed, emotional, fragile but underneath it all, ferocious. The missing brother was more like an appendage than a member of the family. The void created by his absence was even more painful than the finite truth of death.

Most of the men I know are chicken-shit scared of death (present company included). Not R. He was convinced death is another planet, an unseen dimension, most likely better than life on earth. At least easier on a day-to-day basis. He was certain his brother was better off. So he grieved for himself, along the lines of, "How am I supposed to do this on my own?"

When he wasn't dabbing away tears, he'd howl with furious rage. He treated his brother's death as an act of wilful desertion. By then I almost believed I'd known the dead man well. Once or twice I caught myself actually defending him, taking sides. Outrageous. Lies formed a web that held me like a numb insect. I think I forgot who I was, gave up on truth or reality, and just clung to each new thread of invention, trying not to fall. Gave up on Self and went with R's momentum.

While I took care of practical things, he spent a lot of time just staring at the ceiling. He could be silent for hours, then come out with some story about their boyhood in Great Whale, so I knew he'd been reliving the past. They'd always been close. Slept in the same bed till they were teenagers. Kicked out of the same school. One talent rode on the other's coat tails. The sibling muses. One's virtuoso violin act kept them both in groceries while the other learned to paint. But as soon as R started making it on his own, the brother-provider hit turbulence.

I suspected that what he let me know about their life was only his version, a chapter-book story told by a wounded individual who in some respects was still a boy. The truth – as they say – went to the grave. So maybe we both falsified, though for different reasons. I'm sure he did. But he's dead and I'm not. His tragedy, my tough luck. So I'll stick to the facts.

While I was still getting used to the air mattress, two facts emerged, clear and brutally relevant: my nineteen hundred something U.S. was almost gone, and R had no obvious means of support. He'd already spent the advance he got for the New Mexico exhibition. As I found out eventually, the exhibition had been postponed because he hadn't painted anything to hang on the gallery walls. Now he was too tired or too discouraged to work. I could have made a withdrawal on my credit cards or simply phoned my erstwhile business partner, Vince, but for navel-gazing reasons alluded to above, chose not too do so.

Instead, I woke up one morning filled with resolve to find work. Real work. Employment commensurate with my demonstrable abilities and current identity, the latter being fluid, but not uninteresting. Given the brutal lack of documents and meagre wardrobe, I decided it was pointless to count on my Masters of Business Administration from Harvard, my partnership in a dynamic independent investment firm, or my many lucrative consulting contacts and fast friends. I would look for something that fit my new look. So I trotted off to the national (un)employment centre (convinced, deep down of course, that I didn't really need work, all a bit of a joke really).

In this advanced state of irony, keeping a self-satisfied smirk just below the surface was a challenge. Alas, I apparently claimed expertise in too vast an array of menial jobs and was immediately pegged a liar. Or, maybe it was attitude. What passes for self-confidence in one milieu can be stricken down as dementia in another. Without wishing to get into the labyrinth of social/political issues inherent in a white man's Red Like Me experience, I will say that the bullshit appropriate at one socio-economic level cannot ipso facto be brought to bear on another. Clearly, native people have to forge their own bullshit. This, I would suggest, is their only hope. Either that or they must resolve to spurn the game altogether. A noble choice, beyond my imagination.

Eventually, I ended up in a warehouse shifting heavy boxes but by noon my back had snapped, and they sent me home.

The last thing a scum boss wants is tangling with Workman's Compensation. He paid me for the entire day. I went down to Value Village, bought myself a cheap suit and shirt, thinking the only real hope was typecasting. Sales, what about sales? Surely a generic talent, with wide application. I bought a newspaper and got myself a couple of interviews. Within a week I was hired to sell shoes on Robson Street. Getting the nod was actually a thrill. Boost to the old ego and a damn good joke, or so I thought at the time.

My two colleagues on the job were jejune vixens with attitude bursting out of their sprayed-on pants. They couldn't believe the manager would take on an aging scarecrow, a man old enough to be their pimp. (A note of bitterness?) Previously, my experience with excessively young women had been restricted largely to tip-tuned barmaids, so I was taken aback. However, their unwelcoming attitude had one positive side effect: it provided motivation. I soon discovered a hidden talent for selling comfortable walking shoes to women old enough to be my mother. These older ladies instinctively shunned the harpies, and made a beeline straight for me. Older women were not particular about the product and never in a hurry. They clearly enjoyed the brush of a man's hands on their ankles. So be it. I did not hold back. Shoes flew off the shelves.

One afternoon, out of the corner of my eye, I caught sight of a frizzy perm atop a hound's-tooth car coat, fingering the Dr. Scholl's. It was as if lightening had struck: a heart-stopping jolt, immediate wave of shame and guilt, forced surrender.

I walked up and said good afternoon, fully anticipating my mother's snarl of response. She was not, of course, though from behind, the resemblance was frightening. She had the same ragged steel edges, but fortunately was *not* my mother.

Mother, the warm, angelic presence in my childhood. But cold and critical when it mattered most. From about the age of fourteen, everything I did or said was WRONG. How could she have known? We hardly spoke. Couldn't figure it out. Why she turned mean. Even after I left for Harvard, barely a smile. Years went by, I found myself wishing the old man were alive, so I could ask his opinion. Man to man: what's ailing your wife? What happened? The chill of old age? Or is it something I said? (A stretch of expensive therapy revealed her frosty withdrawal may have tainted my ability to forge a lasting bond with a woman. Fascinating. Fascinating. Could even be true, though suspicion hovers around a thousand other reasons.)

Then the fiftieth birthday party. A knock at the door – that's all it took and suddenly the mystery was gone. The secret that ate into her, year after year, was revealed that night, to all who wanted to see. Even before I was told (or figured out) who he was, I knew *what* he was. The missing puzzle piece. Neil: the first fish, caught too soon, thrown back. I followed him into the kitchen that night, saw the muscles in her neck tighten when he looked at her. She leaned forward for a better look, shed all evidence of dementia. Her face lit up. She knew him. *Because she had been waiting*. Every minute of every day and night for decades, she had been waiting for the moment when her first born would walk through the door and save her soul.

I do not judge. Evidence of passion in one's youthful parents is surely a cause for celebration. But why were we not told? A bastard son given away at birth would of course come back to claim his due. Let him have it! The times, blame the times. Instead, we, the pampered wanted ones, were forced to wait in limbo. We swallowed her secret. Amanda, me, and the poor stooge cuckold. Yes, a medieval term is appropriate here. Her ignorant husband – my father – never knew why he spent his life with a woman who was ABSENT at every crucial moment. If he had lived long enough, I would have asked him face to face, tell me dad, when you fucked her, where was she? Mentally? Emotionally? Far, far away, right? Well now we know where. This much is clear: a huge part of my mother, his wife, was somewhere else. Amanda may have remained oblivious, she had concerns of her own. But the old man – he was the loneliest son of a bitch on the planet. Lonely in his ignorance, which even his pubescent, self-obsessed only son could not ignore. Lonely, because he lived in a house of lies. Sub-zero, silent, empty house, because her love was somewhere else. Gone, given away, taken away at birth.

The problem is, I knew. Me, the invisible one, I felt it in my gut. Did she imagine her gullible sponge of a second son would fail to notice? I sensed her lie every day of my life. Her existence unsettled my belief in truth. Because we had so little of it at home!!! Neil is the walking proof of that. Every time she looked at me she thought of him. I was the lightening-rod child through whom love passed but did not stay. I was invisible to her. Like the old man, duped into lifelong worship of a liar.

And suddenly I was expected to meet him at a contrived "reunion" set up by Amanda (who is a sucker for *Reader's*

Digest-type stories that hang on the paperback best-seller lists for months. Never to be confused with reality. Or literature.) Amanda and Tom and Neil and – what was her name? Wendy? Wanda. At some restaurant – one big happy family. Too easy, too fast. Sorry, I am not American, I do not heal and weep, spin on a dime, in time for Oprah's next commercial.

So I ran, but not from the truth. I went directly to the source, to my mother, who I suspected was far from senile. I wanted to hear her side of the story. Unfortunately (though not perhaps surprisingly) she had chosen to sink back into the stupor. Her final ruse. She hardly knew my name (if she had ever known or seen me). So I did not waste my breath asking her questions.

Instead, I took the time to survey old home-movie footage from select family events, Christmas especially, and I found evidence of the lie, captured for eternity. A far away look; she simply was not there. Eyes fogged up, no doubt dulled by common suburban tranquillizers. This is how I finally *finally* came to know my mother. Who she was, and why. Yet knowing does not stop me from wishing I was Neil – the one she longed for – instead of me, invisible.

(Preceding statements: totally unreasonable. Raving rant of a selfish mind. In a forthcoming sanitised/sane version of this present spiritual odyssey, all comments making the Author look weak or self-indulgent or needy will be stricken out, reworked as positive insights into character.)

I love my mother deeply and long to see her again as soon as possible, before she dies.

IV

WINNIPEG. One-hour stop. Brief sortie to size the place up, test my legs.

After forty-two hours on the train, walking on land felt like stepping across a waterbed. On every street corner, there was somebody who looked like R. Moon-shaped faces, shoulders wrapped up in blankets. Men and women lingering, sitting on the sidewalks, staring glaze-eyed or drunk and ranting. And others of the same people, on the move, clutching cell phones, right at home in the urban blur. Fixating on the women would be easy. Native girls – dark eyes, cheekbones, skinny bums, exquisite. Staying in Winnipeg was tempting. Made it back on the train just in time, armed with an unbreakable micky of Canadian Club. Transconna – Elma – Brereton Lake – Ophir – Winatoba. This train stops every half hour, sometimes in the middle of a field. Passengers leap out of nowhere, or get off and disappear into the bush. Powerful urge to follow; instead I sit tight and scribble, drinking CC by the capful.

The shoe-sales job ended after Boxing Day. I regretted missing the January sales, thought we could have moved those beige pumps in a weekend or two. As it turned out, I was cut loose just in time. R was sicker than I thought, and took a turn for the worse, requiring several midnight trips to the Emergency room, blood transfusions, oxygen.

Doctors vague as to what was ailing him. I suspected the worst and confronted them, which is how I uncovered the widespread assumption that R and I, his houseguest, were a couple. Honestly, it hadn't occurred to me he was gay. My erstwhile business partner Vince is, too. Which hasn't stopped him from being a financial shark, or coming on to the occasional baggy heiress when necessary. So what? I realise it looks bad in print to insist I didn't care; looks like I did but I'm making an effort to cover it up. Well, the truth is worse – I didn't notice.

Anyway, I was deeply relieved when the doctor proclaimed his patient showed no trace of HIV. Nevertheless, he seized upon the opportunity to suggest that R and I stop doing whatever it was we were doing to each other, just in case. Under normal circumstances I would have protested, explained the situation. But it didn't seem worthy of effort. One of the many perks of being 'dead.'

Odd though it seems in retrospect, as soon as I heard he wasn't carrying the plague of the century, I became convinced R would get well. Around that time, it began to matter very much that he would recover. I knew I did not have the intestinal fortitude to witness, let alone play bartender to a physical ordeal. I'm weak, basically, a moral coward. Tender stomach, I definitely prefer pleasure to pain. All trace of ancestral puritan fortitude has been lost on me, filtered out by a bourgeois upbringing, high IQ and a keenly developed understanding of futility, the latter a genetic gift from my maternal grandfather, Frank Woodhouse. Thinking of gentle Grandpa Frank, I have to add the too-often-overlooked power of inertia. I did not choose to stay with René until the end. He dug a rut and I fell in. Or, he hooked me and I decided not to notice.

I'd have run if I'd known what was coming, but just in time, he handed me a hit of hope. The fever broke. He got up one morning and announced he was about to start a new painting. This, after swearing on his brother's (non-existent) grave that he would never paint again, that he could no longer stomach even thinking about Art. So, I thought, he's changed his mind. This is good.

I was taken by the idea of watching him work. But no, he swore he could not pick up a brush unless the room was empty. Therefore, I was out on the street.

He'd start about ten, ten-thirty, work through until the sun went down, subsisting on Cheezies and gallons of Earl Grey tea. The picture grew by fits and starts, sometimes moving ahead for a few days running. Then I'd come in and find huge patches painted over with white. He said nothing is ever lost in painting. Not even time. It's all there, lurking underneath, doing battle with the bits that stay on top. After a couple of weeks it looked to me like he was almost finished – a huge, beaked creature with a mask and skinny legs danced in the foreground, against a surreal landscape crowded with florescent pines and skyscrapers disappearing into toxic clouds.

Then came the great setback. His gallerist dropped by, the guy who'd picked him up after he'd been tossed out of the highest echelons of the art world for failing to service his master. Even I could see this was a B-list kind of person, a pointy-chinned rooster in shiny, stove-pipe pants and a floral shirt unbuttoned half way down to his navel. He brought a bag of oranges and a box of chocolates, nice gesture but lost on R.

I hid in the can while the encounter took place. The visitor crowed over the work-in-progress, being especially pleased that R had tackled a Big Piece of Canvas. He was at a point in his career where size counts. If you're nobody, you can't give the big ones away; once you make it, small will do. In the meantime, big paintings fill big spaces, which mean large homes and offices, lobbies, hence, rich buyers. They always needed big expensive paintings, so the investment would be obvious.

The rooster loved what he saw, predicted a quick sale. He wanted to bring the prospective collector by, but R declined, saying too much exposure would throw him off course. So the rooster agreed to be patient, though his parting words included a few shots that sounded more like threats. Apparently the New Mexico exhibition was hanging in the balance. He agreed to sell this one painting to pay for food and drink, but only if he saw definite signs of work on the forthcoming show. The drug of hope. Listening from behind the toilet door, I imbibed.

After he'd gone, R threw himself on the mattress and cursed. When I came back that night, half of what he'd had on canvas had been painted over, lost in cloud of revisionist angst. I blew up, started yelling, called him a childish, spoiled brat. Did he think I'd support his navel-gazing forever? First and only time I ever lost it in his presence. R stayed uncharacteristically calm, even managing to mumble faint repentance. Said he appreciated my honesty. The one thing he couldn't stomach was praise. Of course I felt like a complete cretin asshole and spent hours cooking an apology, which he wolfed down without a word.

He stayed in bed late the next day, then got up, mixed a few new colours, and went back to work.

For the next few weeks, we moved like sleepwalkers through a set routine. As noted, R was utterly ignorant of – uninterested in – things practical. Where did that bag of groceries come from? Never once did he wonder out loud. I'd fry up a plate of eggs, he'd shout out "sunny side up," and glare at the plate if he didn't see bacon. *Did you smell pig grease?* Strange as it was, I embraced the role with all the zeal of a life-long *Chatelaine* magazine subscriber. Even had a go at the rusty toilet bowl, territory hitherto tended by hired help or women with nesting ambitions. Part of it was lack of anything better to do. And R was so frantically, contagiously busy. By the end I was a slave to his disintegrating body, but there was a time in between where art ruled. Thinking about it now, I guess that was the hook. He got up from his deathbed to paint. Who would have walked away from the fury of hope?

On the surface, at least, my outburst over the spoiled masterpiece arose from a practical source. We were broke. R said it was my fault. He said the gallerist had assumed I – the "houseguest" – would be paying our way, and so had refused to give him another advance. What about your friends? I said. Couldn't you borrow? This brought on laughter. He said his so-called friends had all deserted him when he got kicked out of the top gallery. Except one, Lucky, a Cree medicine woman. She was temporarily out of town, "Don't worry," he said, "she'll be back in time."

At least once a week, he'd journey down to the bank machine to try his card, as if expecting cash from some vague source. He was usually disappointed. If I said anything about leaving, he'd throw himself into a coughing fit.

When he did get a few dollars, he'd spend it immediately on whatever culinary treat caught his eye. I wasn't quite as comfortable with an empty belly. Tended to think ahead, caught myself once or twice going through his pockets for loose change, which I stashed away for a lean day.

During this time, I became frugal to the point of obsession, a veritable pocketbook anorexic. I started to notice that 99 per cent of all products edible or otherwise were vastly overpriced. When you've always had money and suddenly don't, resentment sets in fast. Mine soon built to a powerful grudge, which loosened normal inhibitions, leading naturally to shoplifting. A tremendous thrill the first time round, it soon got me tossed out of two major supermarkets. (Note to novice criminals: practice in middle-class suburban malls. Pros have ruined the Downtown Eastside for beginners.)

I won't dwell on the humiliation of getting caught with a tin of marinated clams in my coat pocket. Suffice to say, the experience pissed me off, turned me against the poor. Having failed at petty crime, I refused to sink further, to compete for meaningless employment alongside the lower echelons of society. Instead, I resolved to soar above ignominy with a masterful scheme: I'd return to my original plan, and write a screenplay.

Under the circumstances, the ideas I'd worked on so far seemed ludicrous: a grudge-settling mud bath based on divorce? A winsome road picture flattering the blind? Ensconced in the lower depths of East Hastings, I realised the only movie worth making would be searing social commentary – a satire, with comic overtones, about a disgruntled stockbroker who takes up panhandling. By then I'd watched bums at work. I figured all I had to do was organise a plot and type up the visuals. This concept would be cheap to shoot – half the Downtown Eastside population would be hired as extras. They could wear their own clothes.

So, I purchased a used briefcase and pad of lined paper. As often happens when you embark upon a new obsession, omens appeared, and drove me on. I came across a well-thumbed copy of George Orwell's *Down and Out in Paris and London* which I'd dipped into as an undergrad and dismissed as an Oxford dandy's dalliance with poverty. A twenty-something would-be writer's search for material – contrived, I thought then, his travails in the brutal slog of Paris restaurant kitchens.

Reading it again, slowly, I discovered quite another book. Sure he could have written home for money. He did, eventually. Just as the poor could drag themselves up out of their rut. I could have bolted on René, or exercised other options. Even now I wonder why I didn't. Maybe I could have saved him, a heart-breaking thought. Could have? No, untrue. Life is a moment – that much I know. I lived the moment, coped in my own ludicrous way.

Hunger was real and present. So I decided to research my movie, and in the meantime, raise enough change for supper. Thus, wrapped snugly in irony to protect me against mortifying embarrassment, I planted my cowboy boots on Robson Street and stuck out an empty paper cup.

The first few minutes were disastrous. I couldn't stop laughing. Nobody gives money to a laughing man with a brief case at his heels. Very few give to a desperate man who looks them straight in the eye and pleads. Subtlety is vital, especially from a fifty-year-old bum, the most common and least appealing category of beggar.

Mid-way into the second day of 'research,' I was bored out of my mind, eager to tackle the screenplay. How much could there be to learn? I had, however, netted $31 in just under five hours.

The following morning, I spent slumped over an empty page at the Vancouver Public Library. At noon, I spent $7 on a soggy tuna sandwich and machine coffee to keep myself (not) working. Annoyed by the outrageous expense, I drained the cup and resolved to recoup the loss before getting back down to my masterpiece.

As it turned out, panhandling was a lot easier than writing a screenplay. Anyway, the money was immediate. At first, the delusion of research kept despair at bay. Then I started to get used to it. Then I resolved to get good at it.

One sure thing about being a bum: you're close to invisible. Most people turn away. A few glance at you, either speed up or fish into their pockets for change. Occasionally somebody stops to talk, which was excruciating. I never got a cent out of conversation. A few words from me and the most resolute Good Samaritan would leave in a huff.

The only way a middle-aged white male can score as a beggar is to put his whirling mind on ice and give in to abject destitution. Keep saying to yourself, over and over, you are finished, shit, guilty, let it all go. Confess and fire all lawyers. Throw yourself at humanity's feet. With that thought on your face, other males will identify desperation and toss you a buck, thinking, "There but for the grace of God go I." Women will show pity. Maybe you remind them of their ex-husbands, of where they deserve to be. I watched younger guys succeed with witty, hand-drawn signs and musical instruments. That's not what pedestrians expect from the older poor. Traces of humour are always taken badly. You're down and out. Embrace it.

Theoretically, at least, it wasn't really me. The hunger was real, but I knew I could escape. And yet the rhythm of it, standing inert in the cold, watching people with cash whirling by, hoping they'd stop – it tightens you on the inside. Damp or something settled into my bones. Maybe I wasn't faking. I was destitute. I sank into inertia. Incredible fatigue. One afternoon I took the first few bucks I got and spent it on liquor and just drank myself into a stupor. Outside, in the street, lay down in an alley and slept it off. This was no Orwellian fantasy, nothing experimental. It welled up in me, sadness. Waste. Monstrous misunderstanding.

Around that time I saw this scribbled on a toilet door: "Happiness is so easy. Why don't more people go for it?"

A thought like that can bring you close to despair.

In the time I knew him, R never left the four-block radius of his loft, though he loved to glorify life in the bush, raved about it in the middle of the worst. Once, when he couldn't sleep for more than an hour or two at a time, he told me about the hunting trips he'd taken with his uncles and the late great brother. Then, out of nowhere, he started cursing the departed, blaming him for dying, and I said, "Lay off, you're lucky you had a brother."

For once, he actually listened to me.

"You don't have one?"

"No," I said. "Not really."

He sat bolt upright in bed. "What you mean 'not really?'"

I shrugged.

"You're holding back on me, Heartless. That isn't kind. After all we've been through. I take you in off the street, give you free rent, and then you sit there and say something crazy like you didn't *really* have a brother. What, did he die?"

So I said, "Worse. My mother had a baby when she was seventeen, and gave him up for adoption."

He laughed.

It stung. I said, "Glad you're amused."

He said there was a steady flow of accidental babies raised by aunts and grannies of his tribe. That was hardly reason to disown a brother. "So, you have a brother. Say it: 'I have a brother.'"

At the time, he weighed about 102 pounds so there was no question of punching him. Instead, I said nothing, which he hated.

"Don't ever hold back on me, Heartless. Not in these circumstances."

Believing the best defence is offence, I said, "What about you? Aren't you holding back on me?"

"What do you mean?"

"I mean I think you enjoyed mixing with the art world perverts. Hmm? Maybe you're not telling me everything?"

I'd intended to tease, not punch him in the gut. It slipped out. He was feeling strong that night, and we were drinking. He fought back.

Once he got started he couldn't stop. The story spun off in many directions. At first I thought he was mocking me. Weird fables about Tricksters and hoards of mythological characters, stories involving himself and his brother as kids, superhuman exploits, straight out of bedtime books. He saw me smile and kept right on. Bit by bit the fairy tale centre of his boyhood disappeared. The baroque adventures of two hearty boys morphed into cryptic anecdotes, and for a while I though he was relating a nightmare or I'd lost the thread. Working hard to keep it bubbling, keep the story moving, he mixed myth with memory, and started telling me what really happened.

It was not a simple tale of two brothers whose great talent brought them money and fame. Their pact with devils began at a tender age. They were too young to have experienced the notorious residential schools, where boys risked becoming sex toys to senior perverts. But the kindly art teacher who showed them the road to creativity was a bona fide graduate of the worst of such abuses. Unfortunately, he'd gained a taste for unequal encounters. R and his brother caught his eye.

When he told me what they'd had to endure, he garnished it with gutter vocabulary so that it seemed almost distant, except that as he went on, his voice would slip into another registry, become a kid's voice, like he was back there when he remembered. The change in his voice always, always made me choke. This was the source of his eternal youthfulness. He was frozen. Stayed the boy. He'd built a few layers around the hurt but it was there just the same.

NORTHERN ONTARIO. There is something godless in this landscape. It's haunted with spirits unknown to the likes of Self.

Night falls. Enough.

No, push on, remember more. Where it led.

One night, shortly after his ultimate confession, things came to a crisis, so to speak. We were asleep, me on my air mattress, he at the other end of the room. I felt a presence. Leaped up, turned on the lights. Found R on all fours, crawling under my covers.

"What are you doing?"

He curled up, sheepish.

"I want to make you feel good," he said.

"You can't."

"Yes, I will."

"No."

"Give me a chance to love you, Heartless."

"Get away from me."

He wouldn't move. I got my coat and started for the door.

"All right," he said. "Forget it."

I opened the door.

"Come back!" he shouted.

"No, do your own fucking dishes."

He was kneeling in the middle of the room, gazing plaintively. "Why are you punishing me? Have you never tried to love somebody who didn't want it?"

"Yes, I have."

"What happened?"

"She slapped my face."

"So?"

"So don't touch me again."

"You hate gays."

"I do not."

"You do."

"No."

"Have you ever done it to a man?"

"No."

"Had it done to you by a man?"

"It? What?"

128

"You know what I mean."

"Yes."

"Yes, like you did it?"

"Rather, I had it done to me."

"Who?"

"A certain hockey coach."

"Did you like it?"

"Not particularly."

"Did you tell anybody?"

"No."

"But you quit hockey. Is that why you stopped playing?"

"No . . . Well, maybe."

"You were scared? Did he threaten you?"

"No. I threatened him, so he stopped. But . . ."

"What?"

"I figured I was being punished, or something."

"For what?"

"Lying," I said. "I used to lie all the time. I told my sister terrible lies. Then I went into her room one night and told the truth, but she didn't believe me. Don't ask me any more questions. That's all I know."

"Okay, okay," he whispered.

Until that moment, the reason I had felt compelled to confess to Amanda had remained a mystery. He cracked me open. Having a grown man, the coach, rough me up had made *me* feel guilty. So I tried to make amends, somehow. Lord knows what Amanda thought I was up to.

That's the effect R had. He held me down and squeezed out secrets I'd kept from myself.

V

DAWN. Somewhere in the wilds of Ontario. Hornepayne. Oba. Alsace. I kid not. Vertebrae a rigid chain of rebellious bones, white hot from the pain of sleeping on the floor.

Surprise: dreamt of Vince last night, dear oily Vince and his latest conquest, Angèl, a strapping masseur from Peru. Sees him once or twice a week for deep thumb work. (Or did. May have moved on by now.) Vince tried to talk me into a full body massage, only eighty bucks an hour. Said I could write it off as a business expense, and Angèl really needed the work. Although straight, I am completely comfortable with Vincent's alternative sexual orientation, however, have no wish to experience caress of my aching spine by hands that have been all over my business partner's piston. Is this homophobic? Possibly, but I don't like heights either.

Or the thought of being buried in a box. Scatter what's left. Had my lawyer put that up front in the last will and testament. Speaking of wills: supposing I am officially dead in Montreal, this would mean Vince owns the business outright. Such was the deal. Two heirless moneymen got drunk one night and decided to take out insurance policies on each other, so to speak. Survivor takes all. (Ultimate expression of trust between two men: betting X won't succumb to the temptation of having Y killed, or vice versa. Caveat: the fine print specified: in case of death from natural causes.) So Vince is king – for the time being. Chances are he's moved into a more aesthetically pleasing office space, redecorated. Won't he be surprised to see me?

NOTE: My first positive thought of Montreal is a wicked one.

I stink and I know it. This sleeping bag will be burned upon arrival.

Resolution: under no circumstances go back to the lunatic world of money management. Sub-resolution: bear in mind that poverty is bad, bad for the world and up-close-personal bad for H. Granger, who is too old to be poor. Grateful to destiny for the experience, and thirty pounds thinner, but basically fed up with scraping by as a way of life. Is this back-sliding from lessons learned? No.

Further resolution: find a *use* for whatever remains of natural life, a way to contribute to the world. Must not lose raw lucidity, as the train chugs closer-closer-closer to my long-lost life.

I will give back to society, after covering basic expenses.

Paradox of a good man's exit from this life . . .

Finally, a diagnosis: cancer. He declined hospital treatment. As the beast grew stronger, R fought back with raging fits of lucidity. He did not go gently. I was the sponge. Dart board. Whatever. In the dark days, he forgot what he'd told me, sparse details whispered in confidence. He re-told the same stories, spilling out guts and gore, denouncing the guilty. The abuse, stuff he and his brother had been up to. I've seen a bit of the pay-as-you go world, especially in Thailand, but he's lived nights *in Canada* that made me shiver. Enough. He does not deserve to be remembered by the things that shamed him.

Shame: panhandling. Started out as a lark, research for a movie I still intend to write. Eventually became a refuge, means of escape from the sick room. Told myself I'm doing this for him, raising funds to get him better painkillers.

Two weeks ago, as he'd predicted, a big woman named Lucky came by with medicines – herbs, unlabeled pill bottles, and (no joke) small brown balls that looked and smelled like rabbit droppings. I never had the guts to try any of them, but the effect on René was impressive. Better than morphine or dope. Pain seemed to evaporate. He usually fell asleep smiling, but sometimes the opposite, a burst of energy. He'd sit up with his arms folded, insist we talk.

In a desperate effort to keep his attention, I proceeded to divulge the dirty ways and means of an entrepreneur who makes his living from other people's money. (He laughed at this, citing my paltry panhandling income. *Was*, I said. "Money *was* my medium. I've given all that up! Just like you gave up painting your masterpiece." That quieted him down.

The thing that drives a person to pursue a talent is no more obvious than his reasons for giving up. Amanda remains convinced I've squandered mine. Wrong. The making of money out of money is the sine qua non art of our time. It's the only medium still open to a white middle class male – his predecessors having pretty well scaled the summits of music, painting, literature, poetry, even cinema, circa Twentieth Century. I've made and lost millions from almost nothing, using improvisation, vision. This was my contribution to civilisation.

Those days are over. A point completely missed by R. He insisted we start immediately, take up the true art of making money. (Come to think of it, this was one of the few times he actually clamped onto something I said about myself.) I assured him money was wicked, and we would both go straight to hell if we even entertained a partnership.

I described every scam I'd ever used and some I'd even personally invented to separate hapless bread-earners from their savings. Oh yes, some of them made money from us, but suffice to say, we never lost. He'd glaze over when I went too deeply into technical details, but wherever possible I took the time to flesh out the human component; that got his attention.

Money is basically a game, I explained. The goal is satisfaction, which of course money can never deliver. So the job of a money manager is to keep the investor's thoughts focused on the future, when he or she will be infinitely richer than now. Such being the case, it is irrelevant whether he or she has made or lost money in the past year, years or decade. What counts is a vigorous prediction of the future. Of course, some don't listen. They just wander away, buy bonds, and you never hear of them again. But there are always new people walking through the door. That's the secret of our success. Keeping the door open.

To which R said, "Yes, but all of these people you worked for, they're still rich no matter what they lost? Aren't they? Nobody's sleeping in the street or starving."

"They grow depressed and jump off tall buildings," I said.

"No they don't."

"Some do. The sensible few."

"You are one cynical son-of-a-bitch, Heartless Granger."

Yeah, but inside every cynic is a screaming romantic.

When he didn't have the strength for words, he'd take a magic marker and write on my hand: TALK, meaning, tell me again how he died. Show me again how he danced himself to death. From the few sounds I could remember, he reconstructed the song and filled in the missing words. At first he said it was a brave and ancient war chant. Later he said it was the words to "Silent Night." I didn't know what to believe.

Chi-i ya mow / Ti-i pi skaw / No gon A / wa sa yach / Agota. Ni ya / na ka chi ach / A pish Ta-a wash / A ni pa yich / A chi yam Mi kwa mo yich / A chi yam Mi kwa mo yich.

An emaciated ex-stock/money-man learns traditional Cree dance steps by following bedridden commands from a dying master. Ludicrous in the telling, but R did not laugh. He cried. The dancer maintained ironic distance and therefore did not experience shame at the time.

Thinking about it now, I cringe. The fog is lifting. Soon all that happened will be lost. So don't skip over . . . I danced.

Yes, I danced. *A chi yam Mi kwa mo yich. A chi yam Mi kwa mo yich.*

Writing it down just now, I chanted out loud. Dark heads in the next seat looked over, exchanged faint smiles. They know the tune. *A chi yam Mi kwa mo yich. A chi yam Mi kwa mo yich.* They chant back. Our voices combine. Then I let it go, withdraw into memory.

No, those shameless nights waiting for death will never be forgotten.

Too weak to go on, he gasped: "Talk. Talk talk talk!"

A mercy gesture, I talked to keep him calm. Sat by the bed, arms folded and talked a blue streak of fake fiction bilge.

Invented a life to keep him happy. Not quite true. Embellished a life, that's more like it. Walk a mile in another man's shoes and your own won't fit any more.

At the time, the lies I told left a faint acrid taste in the mouth. Looking back, it's the truth that stings now.

R could listen for hours without opening his eyes, then sit bolt upright and scream at me over some minor contradiction: YOU SAID YOU ALWAYS PLAYED GOALIE. WHY WOULD THE BOSTON BRUINS TAKE YOU ON AS A FORWARD????? YOU LIE, HEARTLESS GRANGER. YOU LIE. YOU NEVER PLAYED FORWARD FOR THE NHL.

Caught red-handed stealing my long-lost half-brother's moment of glory!! That was a low point. But it irked me, it really did. To find out he had played for the Bruins. I've come far enough to admit that much.

Naturally, I snapped back.

"All right then," I howled. "You want the truth? I'll tell you the truth: I barely set eyes on your goddamn brother. We shared a hospital room for a few hours. During most of that time, one of us was asleep. This much is fact: I witnessed his last bowel movement, then he passed out on my bed. When I woke up he was gone. DEAD. Taken away. That is the extent my friendship with your wasted brother."

He sat up in the bed, rigid.

"What?"

"You heard me. I did not actually KNOW your brother."

"Why did you say you did?"

"I didn't, you made assumptions."

"You talked about his music."

"*You* talked about his music."

"You told me so many stories."

"I did."

"You said he was great."

"I'm sure he was."

"So you lied."

"Somewhat."

"Why?"

"Because you wanted it. You needed it." I hated to admit such paltry motives.

He tossed back the covers and sat on the side of the bed. His legs were hideous bamboo shoots. He coughed.

"What did he really look like? How did he die?"

"I don't remember."

"You do!" he shrieked.

"No, actually, I was offended by the shit storm. Then I fell asleep."

"Heartless Granger you break my heart."

Then he just folded forward in slow motion toward the floor. Fortunately I was close by and able to break his fall. He was nothing in my arms, a skeleton wrapped in gauze. He clamped onto me like a monkey, long sinewy arms wrapped around my neck. He started sobbing and wouldn't let go when I laid him on the bed.

"Why won't you let me love you? Man to man, love you? It's so good."

"You're too weak."

"Would you if I wasn't weak?"

"Oh yes definitely. We'd go right at it."

"Really? . . . F- you, another lie to make me feel good. F-F-F-F-F- I spray you with F bullets."

Where did he find the strength? I could not imagine.

He said the sickest thing about me was my pathetic need to be loved and liked by all. To be on top of the moment with a good lie, because deep down – under a very shallow surface – I hated myself.

I said, "Okay, there are aspects of myself I dislike, isn't that normal? After a lifetime of living with Self, one is onto one's tricks."

"NO," he snapped. "You must love yourself."

"Do you?"

"Yes!"

"Always?"

He giggled. "Well, I can get annoyed, but I forgive."

"That's the basic difference between us," I said. "You've had things done to you, so you can forgive yourself anything. Mainly, I've done things to others, so it isn't up to me . . ."

"What have you done?"

"I lied."

"To yourself, or other people?"

"Both."

"You lied to people for their own good. The lying good Samaritan."

"Not always."

"So why did you lie to other people, Heartless?"

"To make them suffer."

"Who?"

"People."

"Who?"

"My sister."

"What?!!"

So I told him how I'd tortured Amanda with lies about an older brother named Bill, who'd been forced to leave the house to make room for her.

"So," he said. "That happens all the time in our tribe. Some houses are small."

"See," I said, "That's why you'd make a very poor psychiatrist. Because you've had it so bad. To you, everybody else is basically whining over nothing. It always comes back to you, you, you."

"Why did you want to hurt your sister?"

"That's your department, doc. You tell me."

"So what happened? Did she kill herself?"

"No."

"Is she still mad at you?"

"No."

"Well then what the fff— are you moaning about?"

So I told him how I'd purposely taken a trip to Florida during the last weeks of my father's life, knowing full well I'd miss his final words. Arrived back for the funeral with a gorgeous tan. Mother did her usual broken-hearted routine. She clung to the notion I hadn't realised how sick he was and blamed the doctors.

"You missed his funeral?"

"No, I was there for that."

"What did you miss?"

"His death."

"That's cruel."

"See. I'm mean."

"Are you going to miss my death?"

Once again, the old left hook. I never, ever saw it coming. In all the time we'd spent hanging out at the hospital, the truth had never been spoken.

"No," I said. "I'll stick around for that. How often does a poor white guy get to see a genuine saint kick the can?"

"I want a proper funeral," he said. "Not a bonfire. A box, a hole, grass on top. The whole nine yards." Then he laughed.

"Fine," I said. "But you're not dead yet. So shut up."

SUDBURY. I was not prepared for Sudbury. Train stopped in an industrial park, the middle of nowhere. One hour to take in the sights and smells of mining machinery, and a station like a pre-fab hunting camp. One foot in the bush. Where is Sudbury hiding? No sign of human habitation. I got out anyway, walked down a length of naked highway. Bleak, but the landscape beckoned, unlike Montreal, which at that point had nothing to offer but more of the same.

Gone seven months and who came looking?

Once, I thought I saw Vince on Robson Street. A slim, dapper dude with similar taste in suits. He glanced into my empty Tim Horton's cup and drew back as if from a runny sore. Pivoted and walked away. Yes, that's how Vince would act if he saw me or even by bad luck made eye contact with anyone like me, asking for charity. Vince and his ilk write cheques for tax-deductible donations to causes espoused by people they need or want to know. Always three degrees removed from the needy.

I stood for a while, paralysed, on a roadside leading nowhere, contemplating suicide, or worse. In the shrunken confines of my mind, dreams of trashing Vince gave me the courage to get back on that train and write the rest of this story down. Settling down in Sudbury would change nothing. I cannot run away, even to a rocky paradise that calls out to my graveyard soul.

A live wire connected the back of my neck to the future, stretched tighter with every step. I turned and hurried back to the train.

The ordeal of writing it down had rendered me weak.

LATER. Only two places to get off between Sudbury Junction and downtown Toronto: Parry Sound and Washago. Time is running out. A few hours left to record once and for all R's final days, his final hours. This is hard. I am not up to telling it. The story must tell itself. I am worn down and out.

Ten days ago, R's last Friday. Lucky came by with her usual bag of goodies, plus groceries, toilet paper, a bottle of whiskey. Amazing woman, an old friend, one of his own people. Silent, gentle to the core of her being. Watery, lost eyes and strong hands.

She took one look at him and her face went still. I hadn't noticed. For a week, all I'd done was sit and talk, so naturally I hadn't noticed the change. She pulled up a chair and folded her hands in her lap and bowed her head. Her lips were moving. Must have been in prayer. I poured myself a mug of whiskey. It was late afternoon, the sky still lit up, but cloudy. As we sat there, it began to rain.

She said, "He's burning up."

She got up and boiled the teakettle. Filled a kitchen bowl full of liquid from a bottle she had in her knapsack and warmed it with a bit of hot water. Then she took out a small piece of rough cloth or hide, I don't know which, let it float in the bowl and rolled back the covers, starting with his feet. She washed his body inch by inch and as she uncovered his frame one bit at a time I was horrified to see how wasted he'd become.

I had a flash of the lyrical sister who'd lured me to Vancouver. In the last few hours of his life R looked, yes, like he was dying. But at the same time, he glowed.

I was grateful for the presence of Lucky. She kept me from losing it entirely. Under her silent command, I got hold of myself, sat there quietly behind a poker face. Not a clue as to what she was thinking. No doubt that we'd been lovers. Everybody who knew R thought that. For the record, we weren't.

Still, when she eased the covers up past his thighs and revealed for the first time the brown pouch of dick, half swollen and not a bad size either, I was prepared to feel a rush. You never know. Maybe I am, I thought. Way down under, beneath a life-long effort to chase and lay the female sex, there may be a raving queen aching to break free. Maybe I've stayed here all these months because I wanted desperately to plunge into the backside of a girlish man. Overcome some kind of barrier.

No. When I saw the choice bit, no tingle in the groin. Nothing even remotely like what I felt for the teenage whores of Winnipeg, a spontaneous surge from a place beyond the brain. I could have wrapped my legs around any of them, and disappeared forever.

When I saw him naked and forlorn, the one-eyed man stayed limp.

But that did not stop big gaudy tears escaping, rolling foolishly down. The thing I felt then was a stab of pain, rising in the chest and pressing behind my eyes, hence tears. The brain was numb and could not cover pure sensation with the babble of reason.

Love is a feeling that can be described. In this case, an ache. I ached for the poor gone-bone-bag bugger. Ached for what he told me, what he'd made me do and say, what he'd found inside the shell that turned up on his doorstep, a blathering idiot with lies to tell. Which he knew damn well were lies but expected, nay demanded to hear anyway. So what. Truth: I loved being with him, looking after him. I loved the me I was when I took care of him, however briefly. I am grateful to him for taking my mind off everything else, forcing me to forget and escape self and just live.

Goddammit, I loved him.

R's death was messy, tedious, exhausting, disgusting. It would make a good story if this were it. But this one is about me. Specifically, the part of me that died that night. R bit off what was already dead, chewed, swallowed and puked it out, leaving me a better self for the loss of gangrened bits of the past.

Then he died.

I wept openly, big whiskey tears. I screamed outrage at him for being a selfish son of a bitch, worse than his farting brother. For clocking out just when we could have started a real adventure. Gone into business and made so much money. Whatever he wanted, I would have been game. Posed as artists or seriously taken up tribal dancing and moved to Sudbury. I cursed myself in his name, accused myself of everything he would have said had he had the time and strength to continue cursing me, personally. Lucky chanted under her breath, and washed up the mess.

When I woke up the next morning, sore and still drunk, she was asleep in the only chair, a stiff wooden thing with a murderously straight back. Mouth open, snoring gently. R was covered head to foot in a white sheet. I went out and got a couple of lattes. Lucky made the phone calls.

☞ VII ☜

MEMORIAL

ONE

The Western Transcontinental reached Toronto shortly after nine on Friday night. Hart touched ground gingerly, feeling his way on sea legs down the crowded escalator and up again, into the glare of Union Station. He moved slowly, weaving through the boisterous last rush of commuters, disorientated by the speed and pitch of people on the move. He was travelling light: a sleeping bag, a canvas valise full of old clothes, a dog-eared copy of Orwell's *Down and Out in Paris and London*. A hefty roll of oil paintings would follow by parcel post. His most precious possession he kept on his person, a notebook tucked into an inside pocket of his buckskin jacket.

He had hoped writing would lay René to rest, but the wayward waif was more alive than ever. His voice rang in Hart's ears. The sum total of their time together hung on him like a mournful tune.

As the train moved across the country, Hart had taken no notice of friendships launched, passions ignited, deals struck, bores endured. For three days and three nights he worked in a fever, raising his head from the page only when his thoughts raced faster than the pen. Such odd behaviour on a long journey made him a popular target of conversation. Some swore they recognised a famous writer, others declared the mystery man an eccentric millionaire, a madman, or a criminal in flight. Theories were traded, bets placed. But no one dared break through the force field that held him while he wrote.

Somewhere in the wilds of Ontario, he stopped scribbling. He had more to tell and planned to finish before Montreal, but he won't. Bruised by the telling, in some ways worse than the experience itself, he has reached the limits of confession. From now on, he will live out the karma of a man who has surrendered himself to destiny. He is strolling on a tightrope, eyes fixed on the horizon. What comes next will happen to him like a colourful dream to be lived out later, when he wakes up alone. It is a story he will tell when he is old to anyone who will listen.

He checked his ticket: two hours until the overnight train left for Montreal. Stepping outside the station into the night air, he caught a whiff of spicy sausage rising from the mobile grills parked on Front Street. No sooner did his mouth begin to water than appetite was beaten back by a wave of revulsion, a side effect of enduring deprivation. Eating had become a chore, hunger a nagging voice to be put off or ignored. It was easier that way; a full stomach brought on cramps. Yet the smell of sausage held him. Succulent grilled meat, sizzling animal fat, it reminded him of hockey rinks and camping trips with his father, moonlit nights when they'd had nothing to say and the air was heavy with expectation.

Fleeing memory, he crossed the street, headed towards the Royal York, a place redolent with his old life, when he had taken airplanes and crossed borders and noticed almost nothing. He was still wearing the dead man's jacket, blue jeans and pointy boots. He had added a black Stetson over straggly hair, which was greyer now and left uncut for months. There was nothing casual in his entrance, or tentative. The hotel doorman marked him as traveller from the West, but how far west? The distance could be measured by the confidence of his gait. If the doorman judged, he did not let it show.

Toronto was not Hart's town, though he had fond memories of certain spots and bore the place no grudge. As he gazed at the carpeted steps leading into the foyer, it struck him that nothing could be finer than a hot bath and a single malt in this grand hotel, on expenses, no questions asked. He could have found the downstairs bar with his eyes closed. Sliding into a corner table, he checked his wallet, counted just under a hundred dollars, enough for a month of scraping by, or one good blow out.

Hunger is a lazy beast but thirst belongs to runners, and is harder to escape. He ordered a double Scotch and stacked his change in neat piles beside the coaster. The first sip tasted medicinal, the second made him think of sex, and sex, of Sandrine. Seven months since the last phone call. Looking back, he couldn't help but smile. How fitting, the latest move in their game had been a silent good bye, the dial tone. Where was she now? He was anxious to find out. He pictured running his hands along her naked back, recalling every vertebra between her taut neck muscles and the infinitely more friendly swelling of her rump. It was ages since thoughts like that had come to him and lingered. Desire had fled along with hunger and other lesser needs.

How long had it been? Counting back, he arrived at Venice Beach, the night his once-famous actress neighbour had seduced him with a bottle of Cognac, a clumsy, embarrassing grope in mid-summer. Meaning fall-winter-spring – three seasons of celibacy, neither forced upon on him, nor sought out. It just happened that way. A question of age, he decided. Seek and ye shall find, but after a certain point, seek not and ye shall surely not be found. He sat up straight, thinking, this much is certain: it's time to get back on track.

The second Scotch went down easily. His thoughts lingered on Sandrine. Flashes of Sandrine screaming, throwing things, sobs, doors slamming, images of himself shouting up at her window, broken glass, squealing tires, yes, but sex – he recalled with satisfaction – sex had never been a problem. Foreplay could be scrappy and the aftermath might turn blue, but the actual act of penetrating her lean body, letting go, had always been excellent. How could they have wasted time on meaningless arguments, the gist of which was now quite lost, when the only thing that really mattered – true communication – had been so fine? She was the one woman among many he'd ever been faintly tempted to marry and he had married her, although not without a few misgivings at the time. Misgivings, which looked at from a certain angle, had not been without foundation. Insights come and go, he told himself. But the sheer length of time they'd known each other was real and impossible to duplicate with a stranger, at least in the short term.

All that had happened since their last disastrous conversation, months of revelation and reflection – it felt like years,

exposed the quick nothingness of time. He knew he had
hardly begun to plumb the significance of what he'd lived, the
death of two brothers. At least he understood now what the
Bible meant by "Jesus died for our sins." It was not a reference to some kind of numerical exchange, like a hostage
executed in the name of other crimes. Or nineteen young
men giving their lives for a cause, paid off in heaven with
seventeen virgins each. No, His death was a heroic act of
contrast. He died so that mankind's sins would be exposed
as pathetic, redundant, frankly unnecessary and ultimately
trivial misdemeanours. The vast majority of human sins were
banal. This, he saw, was the tragic soft centre of the human
journey. Meaning, *anything* less significant, less unfair, less
awful than the too-early death of a talented young man was
utterly trivial.

Ipso facto, the following insight: Sandrine deserved better than to be jerked around by a man who lacked the ability to see what an amazing woman she could be – she *was*, and
surely still would be when he found her again. She deserved a
man with the guts to tell her so. This, he decided, had been
his greatest mistake (with Sandrine): that he had failed to
simply cut short her tireless harping/whining/obsessing by
shouting, "I love you, damn it, because you are a fucking great
woman!!!" Women wait forever for a simple statement of love,
while men, assholes that we are (he included his friends)
stay mum. As he drained his glass and briefly contemplated
a third, the world looked piteously simple. He judged himself just barely simple enough to grasp this painfully obvious
truth, and survive. More than survive, he mused, counting
out the exact change. Maybe even prosper. There might still
be time for that too.

Leaving the bar, he snaked his way up the spiral staircase, as dizzy as the carpet pattern yet surprisingly clear headed. This much was settled: Sandrine was and would always be a major, major person in his life. He had at last realised a fact that had for far too long been as obvious as a pimple on the nose. Why on earth would she not respond favourably to a clean, uncomplicated declaration of eternal love from a man she had once talked into marriage? He was sure now that his future lay with Sandrine, and fairly sure of his ability to reclaim that future. The past was, after all, over.

As for doubts lurking under velvet conviction, he treated them to a simple historical fact: their original marriage had been Sandrine's idea. She was a Doctor of Philosophy. All he had to do was steer a logical thinker back to first principles, marry her again and his life would be back on track. Then Sandrine, too, could reap the rewards of his experience. She deserved nothing less.

TWO

The yawning granite Hall of the Provinces was nearly empty by the time Hart entered Union Station again. Scotch and thinking had worn him out. Dreading yet another wobbly binge of upright travel, he asked the ticket agent to book him into a couchette and took out his credit card. The price quoted seemed unbelievably high, almost as much as a first-class hotel room.

He pocketed his card and walked away, thinking he'd persevere, take advantage of the quiet and get down a full account of René's funeral, which had been wrenching, yet full of surprises too. The art scene had turned out in full sartorial splendour. Newspaper reports touted the deceased's accomplishments and bemoaned the loss of a promising young talent. The rooster appeared in a shiny black suit to announce a posthumous retrospective of his late client's last works. Hart was furious. Where were they when the boy genius lay dying? It irked him that his only exclusive claim was to have been René's last friend, although nobody seemed remotely interested.

The seating cars were nearly full. He passed up several empty places beside obvious talkers, and continued on into the sleeping car. The steward was an elderly gent with a routine smile. Judging his loyalties weren't particularly corporate, Hart slipped him a twenty-dollar bill rolled stiletto tight, for which he received a pillow and a nod towards an empty cabin, six bunks crammed into a space the size of a modest walk-in closet. After three nights spent slumped in a reclining chair or sprawled out on the floor, the sight of a mattress, clean sheets and wool blanket looked heavenly. He passed out as soon as his head hit the pillow.

By day, the journey from Toronto to Montreal can be accomplished in under four hours. The night train stretches it out to last until dawn, lurching slowly from one stop to the next, finally pulling over in the wilderness to let time pass. When Hart woke up, the train was stopped. As his eyes adjusted, he saw bars of light on the window. His bed resembled a cage, and for a moment he thought he was in prison. Then a dream he'd been having came into focus.

He'd been running down a sliver of highway, desperate to escape, short of breath and too scared to turn and face the enemies at his heels. The worst of it was, he could feel himself slowing down. He was trapped in a body unprepared to keep ahead of fear. He knew he had to speed up but his feet dragged. He gulped the cool night air, swallowing panic. Like a car running out of gas, his pace slackened. Gradually the sensation of being pursued began to fade. He noticed the pavement was wet. Pools of rainwater caught moonlight, glistening like oval mirrors.

Then he saw the highway stretched ahead for miles, and it hit him that he never could have made it by running. Bracing for a long walk, he set his eyes on the distant tree line, a vista that looked strangely like Sudbury. His rhythm of walking soon settled into a comfortable pace, then became mechanical, and he drifted off to sleep. Sleepwalking in his own dream, he knew his feet were moving underneath, but his mind withdrew from the physical sensation of walking.

Suddenly, from behind, the blast of a horn. It jolted him. He caught sight of a deep rose-red snout inching up on his left, a convertible, late Seventies, Pontiac. Behind the wheel, wearing a kerchief in the style of Grace Kelly, was Amanda, still in her teens but as cocky as she'd grown with success. She slowed the car to a walking pace, and said, "Hop in."

He could tell she was glad to see him, and he was glad to see her. He got in and they sped off toward the horizon. Except that his perspective on the scene stayed behind, as if his head had somehow come loose, or like a camera, pulled back in a dolly shot and craned high into the sky. He actually saw himself and Amanda drive away. Then the credits rolled.

THREE

Amanda had recently purchased a luxury motor vehicle, and it was red. Not a convertible, though, a Mercedes, scarcely one year old and hardly broken in. Tom had heard about it through another lawyer in his firm and they got an exceptional deal. Never in a million years had she envisioned owning a Mercedes. Since Tom's firm had made him a partner, they'd been able to pay down the mortgage on their condo off Park Avenue and acquire a modest country place, but they never bought anything for show, always put comfort and security first. The Mercedes was the one extravagance Amanda permitted herself from her recent, unexpected legacy. They named her Rose. She liked to think of Rose as a kind of memorial to Hart. Fittingly, the first time Rose hit the highway, she and Tom were heading to Montreal, to an event organised in Hart's memory.

They stayed overnight in upstate New York, planning to arrive Saturday morning in time to help Sandrine with the last minute details. Although as with Hart's fiftieth birthday, there was little anyone could do but pretend not to notice the haze of tension that hung on any event Sandrine undertook to organise.

As they reached the border, traffic on Interstate 81 thickened and finally stopped. Six long lines of vehicles were backed up, waiting for clearance. This time a year ago they would have sailed through, but since the terrorist attacks, clearing customs had become a serious hurdle. The delay unnerved Amanda. She didn't like to be reminded there was an international border between the two cities she knew best. Reaching into her purse, she came up with her Canadian passport, and handed it to Tom.

"Let's not confuse them," Tom said. "It's simpler if we're both Americans." So she complied, handing over proof of American citizenship. A practical choice, yet sadly symbolic. She wondered whether this might not be the last time she came to Montreal for family reasons. Her two closest cousins had moved away. With Kitty's death, and now Hart gone, the city was losing its pull. It would always be her hometown, an integral part of who she was, but Tom and the kids were thoroughly American, they didn't share those memories. Soon she would be off her native land's radar screen forever.

Finally, the border guards waved them through, with cheerful salutations reserved for obvious innocents. As the Mercedes rolled onto Canadian soil, Amanda began to cry. Though not the first tears to fall since the news of Hart's death in L.A., this latest expression of her grief included tears for the city of her birth, the loss of a time and a place, the end of an era. As they climbed the Champlain Bridge, catching a spectacular view of urban skyline touching river, she was half surprised to find Montreal still there. So thoroughly was this Hart's town that she could hardly imagine it without him there. Tom reached over and took her hand.

News of Hart's death had reached his family and friends in pieces. Amanda was in Beijing at a publishing conference on September 11. When Tom called to tell her what had happened, it was the middle of the night Beijing time, afternoon in New York. In the panic of an international crisis, she could not get a phone line to L.A. or an immediate flight out of China. By the time she got back to New York, Hart's neighbour in Venice had identified the body and, acting on the deceased's wishes (filed under D for death in his beach house sublet), had seen to his cremation.

Even in Beijing, as she waded through the double shock, Amanda had a powerful suspicion Hart wasn't dead. She did mental cartwheels trying to understand why, but in the end it came down to a simple matter of doubt. She doubted a man like Hart would slip away from life. Sudden death in an L.A beach house seemed incredible. The feeling brought her back to a night when they were kids, he had burst into her bedroom, slobbering nonsense, claiming there was no brother Bill. Never had been, it was all a lie. She hadn't believed him. Not that she thought he was lying, he'd just come up close to an important fact and gone on by. He lacked the instinct gene that protects brainy people from the snake oil truth of dreams. She had the gene, and it told her he wasn't dead.

Nothing in the circumstances surrounding his death had put her mind at ease. No member of the family had seen him dead. His neighbour – an actress, for crying out loud! – had identified the body. She resolved to go to California and find out exactly what had happened. But then her mother's health took a turn for the worse and she couldn't leave the hospital.

A few days before her death, Kitty rallied around and seemed to become her old self again. Amanda spent a glorious, sunny afternoon by her bedside. For the first time in ages, she was the daughter, able to say things that mattered to her and count on a mother's wisdom. Finally she couldn't help it, she blurted out, "Mum, Hart's dead. I'm sorry."

Silence. For a moment Amanda feared her mother was sinking back into senility. Kitty's face crumbled, as though her insides had caved in, sucking juice from the surfaces of self. In a soft, clear voice, almost child-like, she murmured, "Oh. Oh dear. Oh poor dear Hart."

Watching Kitty take the loss like a mother had made his death real. Amanda was forced to consider her doubts had been a fantasy created out of anger, or arrogance. From then on, she accepted his death, though grief came in flashes and did not linger.

She tried to mourn him at Kitty's funeral, but couldn't stop thinking that the news of Hart's death had effectively killed their mother. It was her fault for telling Kitty, but at some level, she was also angry with Hart. Unreasonable, she knew. When Sandrine had called to say she'd obtained his ashes and was planning a memorial, Amanda was anxious to attend. She'd looked forward to the occasion to make amends, to put her middle brother to rest, and catch up on the news from Neil. But as the moment grew closer, anxiety took over.

"I just hope Sandrine understands we're scattering his ashes on Mother's grave," she said. "I won't put up with any of her irrational outbursts. I've taken quite enough."

Tom let the statement slide. He knew better than to comment on Amanda's pronouncements, knew from experience that such statements might be true expressions of how she felt at the time but they were no guide to future actions.

Talking tough was Amanda's way of refilling the vast store-house of good will that made her such a successful diplomat. She was incapable of hypocrisy. Speaking her mind served to drain off anger, so she could face the formidable Sandrine with a genuine smile. He hoped the pattern would hold.

"Anyway, this is probably the last we'll see of her," she sighed.

"Now, now. Don't say that," he replied. "After all, she's family."

"She is not family!"

As they entered the Ville Marie tunnel, he took the steering wheel with both hands, braced for the high-speed cruise through dim light.

"She's ex-family," Amanda continued, calmly. "They were divorced for a very long time. I don't see why she's in charge of this. I wish I'd put my foot down. You and Neil and I could very well have organised a memorial for Hart. He's our *brother*, for Pete's sake. I didn't appreciate what she said at Mother's funeral, either. Really, Tom, you agreed with me, didn't you?"

He paused before answering. "At the time, everyone's nerves were on edge. Your mother was a powerful personality. I think we have to take Sandrine's comments in context."

"Mother never liked Sandrine."

"Yes, that was something we all knew. Still, in her own way, Sandrine made an effort with your mother."

"In her own way, yes she did . . . . All right, I'm sorry. Actually, I'm glad she put this thing together. She said she invited all his friends. That's not something we could easily do from New York. I wouldn't know where to start. So, it's good, yes. I'm glad we're doing this. We all need closure. Still, I'm glad we didn't bring the boys. I mean, it's not a funeral. I don't quite know what to expect. "

Just as Tom was about to congratulate himself for having married a beautiful, consistent woman, she shot him a question.

"Are you going to say anything?"

"What?"

"Are you going to speak at the memorial?"

"Me? About Hart?"

"No! Why don't you say a few words about world peace?"

"Oh. Okay. Hart. Well, I hadn't thought about it."

"We're family, Tom. We knew him. Otherwise, it's going to be bilge from Sandrine and an avalanche of silly jokes from his drinking buddies. I shudder to think."

Tom was already making notes as he spoke. "We did have a few good times,"

She noticed the grin, knew he wasn't likely to elaborate. She'd often wondered about the fishing trips Hart and Tom had taken together with "the boys" from Hart's hockey team. She had trouble picturing her blue-blood star trial-lawyer husband coasting along for miles in a pick-up truck, happily dining on red meat and beer. Tom might have fit in with the Racket Club crowd, whose members were business types from Hart's professional life, but the hockey team was a weird mix of Mafioso rejects, self-employed divorced dads and guys with parole officers for best friends. She wasn't a snob (after all she adored Neil, who was a welder). But those trips taken with the hockey gang were inevitably described as 'legendary.' What did they do? What did they talk about? Details were rarely concrete, and never commensurate with the knee slapping howls of delight attached to the mention of some vague incident.

"Well, I'm going to speak," she said, as they pulled up to the hotel door. "I've been thinking of a few things I know about Hart. It's a shame Neil never got to know him. Just as I gained one brother, I lost another." She started to cry again. Tom gave her a hug, and began to wonder how Sandrine would cope with the emotional bloodletting that lay ahead.

FOUR

Wanda and Neil were waiting at the hotel. Tom had taken care of arrangements, booking a suite so they could all be together. It was a pattern they'd gotten into, and it grated on Wanda's nerves. She never failed to notice how smooth the big-time New York lawyer was about paying for everything. Neil made a point of reaching for the odd bar bill and they let him have it, but she could tell it was just for show. He was boyishly grateful, which made it worse. They had a lot more money so let them pay: that was Neil's attitude. Once, she tried to make up for it by bringing an armload of gifts, ornate table decorations she'd hand-painted in her craft classes, beer mugs, framed prints. Amanda made a fuss but the minute the wrapping paper came off, Wanda could see she'd made a mistake. She beat herself up with shame, yet on another level, she told herself she didn't give a damn what Amanda thought.

She'd gotten over being jealous of her half-sister-in-law, at least as far as Neil was concerned. The news that he had a secret family up in Canada had hit her hard at first. She'd been obsessed with thinking they were on the verge of some kind of affair. It drove her crazy. She took her friend Marie's advice, talked to their minister. He didn't understand, of course. How could he? Neil worked on four church committees. He could do no wrong in the minister's eyes. So she shut her mouth and bided her time. One part of her brain worked hard at pretending to be the perfect, calm wife who had gotten over a bad spell. Meanwhile, the other part was making plans. It might take months, maybe even years to put the plans into action, but her days with Neil were numbered. He didn't know it, or maybe he did. If he did, he certainly wasn't letting on. At least things had been calmer since she made up her mind to get away. Sometimes calmer. Other times she lost her balance and ended up right back where she started. Furious with Neil and whoever else it was that ruined a perfectly good marriage.

Tom caught sight of Neil across the lobby, bounding toward them, arms outstretched. A warmer welcome would have been hard to imagine. Still, he couldn't say he was looking forward to the next two days, living in close proximity with a couple for whom the simplest of big-city experiences would be remarked upon and discussed to death. He had a sudden pang for Hart, for the loss of irony, spontaneity, his wicked if sometimes vicious sense of humour. He missed the patina of uselessness that hung on everything Hart undertook, his contempt for conviction of any kind, he wasn't particular. He was vigorous, spiky, totally devoid of purposeful intent, and yet he had a way of making things happen around him. A side effect of standing still, while others struck poses and defended their positions. Neil, by contrast, was salt of the earth, earnest, generous, full of consideration. As he gripped Tom's hand in a manly shake, then threw his arms around Amanda, Tom found himself thinking that all they had in common was an unabashed love for the same woman. He wasn't jealous, but he was starting to see what Hart had found so objectionable about his long-lost half brother. He was too nice.

He resolved to take a few chances with his memorial remarks, set people straight on sides of the deceased they'd never had the privilege of seeing. For Hart's sake, it wouldn't do to let this event turn maudlin, or worse, wither under the grip of Sandrine's devotion to decorum.

Wanda stayed behind in the hotel suite when Neil went down to greet Amanda and Tom. She said she had to wash her hair, which wasn't true. She'd had it cut and set just before they left Sherbourne, but of course Neil hadn't noticed. As usual, he jumped at every opportunity to get away by himself, at least that's the way it looked to her. Sitting on the edge of the bed, she braced herself for the onslaught of relatives. Neil had picked up a box of Turtles at the duty free shop. She ate one, then another. When the box was empty, she stuck a finger down her throat and puked them into the toilet. For a few minutes she thought she could see the little beasts whole again, swimming for dear life, so she flushed them away and cracked open a miniature vodka from the bar fridge to sweeten her breath.

A lot had gone wrong since Neil tracked down his birth mother. On the plus side, she'd lost a lot of weight. The women at the workout club were jealous and she couldn't say she blamed them. While they starved themselves and worked up a sweat, she grew thin with no effort at all, because real change comes from within. She'd read it in a spiritual self-help book once, but hadn't understood what it meant till it happened to her personally.

She helped herself to the second vodka, and lay down on the bed so she'd be fresh when it was time to leave for the memorial. As she dozed off, her thoughts flew upward. She prayed to the Lord for guidance and fortitude, begged Him to lead her through this event, which meant so much to Neil. She longed to demonstrate her love for the father of their three wonderful children. She asked the Lord to get involved, help her defeat the machinations of Satan who was working hard on the other side. It was Satan who aroused evil feelings about the nature of this blood reunion between a boy who was abandoned at birth, and the arrogant, tight-assed atheists who now claimed him as their own. In her struggle against Satan's advice, she knew she had not always been strong, but she forgave herself. She was sick of feeling bad about giving in to the Devil.

As she fell into vodka dreams, she called upon the Lord to take charge, to accept responsibility for shutting Satan up. With the Lord's help, she would awaken from a refreshing nap on the luxury suite bed (damn Tom's arrogance) and follow with a smile every move the Lord directed her to make. But she would not struggle. She would conduct herself with dignity as Mrs. Wanda Springer, wife of a God-fearing man who'd been raised by Christians. She would do her best, no more, no less. The rest was up to the Lord.

When Sandrine's email about Hart's memorial had arrived, Neil's first thought was to say nothing to Wanda. Make up some excuse and go up to Montreal alone. Better yet, don't even go. This solution he dismissed immediately, knowing Amanda would never forgive him. But the thought of lying to Wanda filled him with dread. He never lied, at least not to Wanda. Once or twice he may have kept mum about something that would have upset her; the longer he was married, the more sensitive he became to the range of things likely to arouse his wife's ire. But an actual lie – she'd be onto him like a pet monkey. Anyway, details of something like a funeral were bound to leak out and then – he hated to imagine.

On the other hand, the idea of taking Wanda to a Granger family event had caused him to break out in a cold sweat. He was terrified she'd slip into one of her fits and embarrass him to hell. He knew how far she could go, and at least the surface reasons for her moods. But he had no idea of the pattern. The least little thing could set her off. Other times, when he'd most expect her to lash out, she said nothing.

From the moment he told her about locating his real mother, she'd taken a dislike to the Grangers. He talked to a minister at his church and the minister said, "Well, Neil, Wanda may simply fear change. Reassure her of your love, and pray."

Which he did, except that Wanda embarked upon changes of her own which (in his opinion, which he kept to himself) had wrought far more serious damage to their happy life than anything he had done by tracking down the woman who gave him life. Wanda claimed he'd barged in on someone who clearly didn't want him. That wasn't true at all. He'd hired a detective to do the digging, but after that, he worked through a social worker, who got a lawyer to write a letter, which Kitty Granger answered personally. She laid out the family set-up, and invited him to get in touch. He didn't show Wanda the letter. He had no desire to discuss this strange new chapter of his life with someone who couldn't understand.

When he answered the phone in their hotel room and heard Tom's New England lilt, his spirits picked up. Leaving Wanda behind to wash her hair was his way of saying, do what you've got to do, woman. He'd said it more than once over the past few months. He meant it. But as he closed the door and headed for the elevator, he knew he was also giving in to his weakest, most desperate desire, which was to spend as much time as possible without having Wanda on his heels. He still loved her, no doubt about that. Think of all they'd been through. He just did not want to be in her presence, at least not until she got used to the way things would be from now on.

Therein lay the real problem. Wanda might never be able to understand why he needed to be accepted by his real mother's family. He hardly understood himself. He knew it had something to do with the mystery of being adopted. There were things about himself he didn't know, and it scared him. He wished he'd been able to talk to somebody. He'd tried his minister, even the family doctor, but neither of them had a clue. They'd both jumped in with pat answers. He hadn't bothered to go on.

Only Amanda seemed to understand. He was sure she felt the same way. He wished he'd gotten to know Hart. It might have been good to have a brother's point of view.

FIVE

There were times when Lenny Rosenthal suspected Sandrine must be on some kind of drug. He allowed it might be the chemistry between them. They could have sex twice a day and still be interested in fondling each other until they fell asleep. He'd thought it would wear off after a few athletic weekends, but he was wrong. Months after he'd first made passionate love to Dr. Lamotte (ironically, on the evening of her ex-husband's death) her response to him was still ardent. There was nothing more arousing to tenure-track philosophy lecturer Leonard Rosenthal than the sight of his research director and mentor with her clothes coming off. In fact, Sandrine was often the one who initiated sex, which was something most of the married men he knew only dreamed of, though they talked about it all the time.

Nevertheless, Lenny knew he had to be careful about their affair. His corner of Montreal, largely English-speaking, was little more than a village set down in the middle of a metropolis. Certain rules applied, and he wasn't entirely sure what they were. It was hardly a hotbed of gossip, nothing like the vibrant bitchiness of certain Manhattan or Boston circles where being on or off a desirable invitation list was based on the quality of gossip you brought to the dinner party table. In his Montreal, word didn't travel fast, but then it didn't have far to go. And once a juicy bit of information got out, it was likely to snap right back and hit you in the face.

He wasn't sure how the Philosophy Department would take to the news of a serious romance between their high-flying international star and a lowly junior appointment. Sandrine hadn't come right out and said, don't tell anybody. But they had never attended a university function together either, or made more than cursory eye contact at staff gatherings. They had acted on tacit understanding, at least until today. Sandrine had made it clear Lenny could stay overnight at her place, wear the suit she'd help him pick out, and – she had strongly implied – be her date at her ex-husband's memorial service. He considered this a major, major step.

As he turned off the shower and opened the bathroom door, the aroma of freshly brewed coffee drifted in from the kitchen, over a melancholy tune, faintly Wagnerian with a hint of spring. He pictured Sandrine in her flowing oyster bathrobe, popping croissants into the oven, humming along with the CD.

Always discreet in conversation, Leonard made a point of extending the virtue to his thoughts. He believed that harbouring ill will toward another person showed on one's face, and it was not a pretty sight. Whereas the wisdom of his tribe counselled stark judgements and bold outbursts, Lenny preferred a calm, WASP-like aura of civility. This is what he loved about Sandrine. Moments that on other people might have looked like hypocrisy, she carried off with impressive conviction, Hart's memorial being a case in point. Not an obvious time to make their love public, yet he was confident Sandrine could pull it off.

Taking his razor from the medicine cabinet, he lathered up his face and allowed himself a rare, unchivalrous thought: "What a joy it is to fuck a woman who is humming as she prepares for her ex-husband's funeral. What an asshole, divorcing a woman like Sandrine!"

While he shaved, he wondered, as he had before, how things could have gone so wrong between Hart and Sandrine. Unlike other women he'd known (albeit they were younger), she never spoke uncharitably about her ex-husband. At first, he'd even been jealous, the way her face lit up when she brought his name into a conversation.

Suddenly, an explanation slapped him in the face: quite possibly Hart hadn't cut the mustard sexually. What man of fifty could? Sandrine was in a class of her own. Of course, aging Hart Granger couldn't cope.

Ironically, it was Hart's memorial that had rescued him from the awkward aftermath of a sexual skirmish. Almost immediately after his death, Sandrine had begun talking about a funeral, at least some kind of event to celebrate his life. It had taken months to track down the ashes, a struggle with international bureaucracy which had given Lenny a perfect opportunity to play the understanding friend, just as planning the memorial had offered an occasion to demonstrate his generous, collaborative self. The payoff from that one phone call had been immense. Looking at his clean-shaven jaw in the mirror, he thought, struggle is futile. The Taoists have it right. Life's greatest joys are the product of timing and generalised merit, a result of being, not of doing. Witness how he had glided effortlessly into a great job and great woman. His time had come. Whereas Hart's, sad to say, was over.

He splashed cold water on his jaw.

A sudden spasm of pain struck below his left ear, so quick and sharp it took his breath away. The tendons in his neck tightened. Clutching the sink for ballast, he closed his eyes. The pain squeezed like a giant hand, then let go. He opened his eyes to a burst of stars. In the mirror, an ashen face glared back at him, the face of Lev Rosenthal, long-suffering ancestor, back from the dead to frown. It is unwise to mock the dead, Lev said, without moving his lips. Lenny blinked and the face was gone. He saw himself, wearing a foolish, star-struck grin.

Turning away, he tucked his balls into a pair of Calvin Klein jockey shorts and reached for a pearl grey silk shirt, thinking he would have to ask Sandrine to tie his tie.

Amanda's refusal to accept the credibility of the identifying witness had delayed Sandrine's plans for Hart's memorial for months. Thanks to Amanda's intervention, the L.A. Police Department got involved, then Canada-U.S. customs, and for a while it looked like the ashes would languish forever in the limbo of bureaucracy. Finally, Sandrine had flown to L.A. to meet the famous actress, who seemed a perfectly reliable on-site witness, and to organise a cleanup of the beach house. She assured authorities the ashes they were holding were indeed the last remains of her late ex-husband. After all, she'd been on the phone to him when he collapsed. Amanda would just have to accept the facts, and move on.

To anyone who would listen, Sandrine recounted the story of how she had taken a frantic call from the dying Hart, a poignant, even tragic version of the truth in which she was left dangling helplessly while the great love of her life expired. If she told the story too often or too readily, to near-strangers and people who simply did not care, it was only to keep the demons of guilt at bay.

This much was true: she had tried to call Hart back after the desperate howl and crash. She had even put the phone on redial. But seconds before Lenny Rosenthal carried her awkwardly, frantically to the bed, she had reached out and turned off the ringer. By the time she remembered to check her messages the next morning, the L.A. Police Department had already left three messages.

Through it all, Lenny had been a brick. His support, his quiet understanding and absolute attentiveness to her needs and moods had come as a pleasant surprise. Transformed by affection and attention, she had begun to imagine that the relay of cold, selfish, navel-centred men in her past had simply been a result of bad timing, and that Hart had been no exception. With Lenny the narrative of man meets woman was supported by context. He was there for her in her time of need, actually at her side as Hart lay dying. He helped her prepare the final adieu, deal with the Faculty Club ballroom at McGill, contact a lengthy guest list and supervise the caterers. They had built their love on a firm foundation of crisis.

As she wrapped his slate-grey tie in a half Windsor and smoothed his pearl collar with her fingertips, she was almost grateful to Hart. Lenny looked stunning in the dark, double-breasted suit she had chosen for the occasion. He was tall, young, yet mature and powerful. Thanks in large part to Lenny, she was looking forward to the memorial.

Virtually everyone who had known or known of the late Hart Granger had been invited to raise a glass of Château Lafitte in his honour. The definitive nature of death offered Sandrine a rare, cloudless vision of her troublesome ex-husband. She was absolutely certain he deserved a first-class farewell.

SIX

Using his coffee spoon as guide, Hart ripped an item from *The Gazette*, folded it into the size of credit card and stuffed it into his pocket. He hadn't noticed the waitress standing over him. "Excuse me," she said, tartly, "These newspapers are for people to read." She held up the Saturday review section. It hung like a skeleton in her hands, gutted of several choice pieces he'd deemed worthy of saving.

"I'd be happy to pay for it," he mumbled.

Stepping off the overnight train into the chilly morning air, he'd headed straight for a coffee shop, intending to get his bearings and kill time until the city he knew woke up. For the first time in months, he succumbed to a life-long habit and read the papers while he ate. Anyone who cared to look his way would have noticed a pale, gaunt figure sitting with his back to the wall, a misplaced cowboy, stranded somewhere between the hyper-cool nonchalance of a true original and an ordinary bum. He devoured the Saturday editions, and went through everything that had accumulated since the busboy's last purge. He was unprepared for what he found.

A twenty-year-old suicide bomber had blown herself up in an Israeli market, killing six, wounding eighty. Canadian troops were getting scorched in Afghanistan. Citizens of Quebec were suing the government for war crimes, claiming an elite Canadian task force in Afghanistan had violated the Geneva Convention by turning prisoners of war over to U.S. authorities without a hearing. Enhanced security at local airports now included armed guards, confiscation of nail files and toenail clippers, the replacing of stainless steel knives (forks and spoons are permitted) with plastic on airlines, and sometimes, full body searches. Armed marshals were occupying first-class seats on many flights, and this was just the immediate war news.

He read on, through reports about the capture of Mexico's chief drug lord, the man responsible for smuggling in 40 per cent of all cocaine used in the U.S. About the meltdown of the Arctic ice caps which was providing an open invitation to smugglers, pirates and terrorists into our unpatrolled North-West Passage. And Washington's plans to develop nuclear weapons suitable for striking at targets such as Iraq, Iran, North Korea and Syria.

Pounding the streets of Downtown Eastside Vancouver, he hadn't had much interest in the outside world. He was on foreign turf, knew he would leave at some point, likely never to return. Time away felt like time out. But this was Montreal, *The Gazette*, moreover, normally a hotbed of deliciously parochial crises. What he found sent shivers up his spine. While he'd been reading Orwell, or amusing himself with randomly chosen pocketbooks rarely worth more than a buck, everything had changed. The new world was dark and freaky. Bleak reports from all corners, pundits scrambling to find fresh synonyms for doom. Their grim consensus made it all look worse. In a think piece on the new climate of public opinion, he read:

"It's much too soon for sweeping historical perspective, but some things are clear. More attention is paid to actual news. It has replaced celebrity gossip on the cable news networks, and ratings are up. A third of U.S. adults are spending more time reading newspapers and a fifth of adults are perusing magazines more, reports a research poll initiated after September 11. Public service is hot. Peace Corps applications are up 39 per cent since Bush called for volunteers in his State of the Union address. More people are seeking jobs at the FBI and CIA."

Then his eyes fell upon a damning phrase, aimed, it seemed, straight at him: "The New Normal says thumbs-up to metal detectors at basketball games, thumbs down to ironic cynicism."

He laughed out loud. *What? No more irony? How ironic.*

Such was the glib thought that slipped into his mind as the waitress stood over him, frowning. She was young and slim, with fine blond hair tied back in a ponytail.

She shrugged. "Did you want your refill now?"

"Sure," he said. "Thanks. Is there a pay phone here?" She nodded to a booth beside the washrooms.

When she'd disappeared behind the counter, he sank back into the pile of newsprint. Buried in the nether regions of information was a long feature on star watching, a boyhood obsession he'd let drop, like so many other passions. He tore out a final selection:

"Many stars in the night sky, when viewed through binoculars or telescopes, have one or more companion stars. Observers can see them if they are bright enough and far enough from their partners. However, sometimes three or more stars are bound together by gravity; these are called multiple-star systems. Locked in their gravitational dance, light years apart, stars may take centuries to circle each other. These faint celestial objects are best observed at the beginning of a new moon, when their shapes and colours can be seen with greatest clarity and impact, without the distraction of moonlight."

Turning to the weather page, he saw the day would be sunny. A new moon had appeared during the night. Another omen, he thought. Time to call Sandrine.

SEVEN

Like his father and grandfather before him, Hart kept up membership in the Montreal Racket Club, an unabashedly Brit-soaked institution founded in the 1800s around a quick, fast game resembling doubles squash, which it inspired. In any given year, less than half of the club's 100 members actually stepped onto the court. The turnout for drinks and talk was much higher, being essential nutrients to the brotherhood of money and power. In true gentlemanly fashion, no one talked business inside the wood-panelled walls, yet the club was all about business – minding one's own, affecting indifference, soaking up essential rumours and demonstrating who was and wasn't still alive.

A stucco and beam building tucked away on rue de la Concord, just below Sherbrooke, the Racket HQ offered its members a full range of amenities. It was the first place Hart thought to go when it dawned on him he couldn't face Sandrine looking and smelling like a bum. He couldn't even phone her until he'd scraped off a layer of stink.

It was still early Saturday morning; he hoped he'd be able to slip in and sneak a shower without being noticed. The club's front door was open. There was nobody in the lounge, no one to ask where he'd been or cast a critical eye on his rumpled get-up, except the portrait gallery of past presidents, blue-chip gents with suitable half-smiles. Their eyes followed him as he made his dash for the showers.

The club steward was catching up his paperwork in a tiny office behind the bar. It wasn't the first time he'd seen one of the boys drop in to lose the evidence of a night spent away from home. He thought he recognised Hart, did a double take, and waited a few minutes before investigating.

Hartford Granger I, Hart's grandfather, had been a dynamic and much-loved club president just after the Great War. His son, Terrance, had been too busy as an ambitious surgeon to take much interest in club activities, though he kept up his dues. When Hart came back from Harvard, he found himself the owner of a five-year membership funded by his grandfather, who wanted his grandson to take social connections seriously. Racket Club members were keenly aware of family background and profession. Bankruptcies, divorces, illness and sundry scandals came and went; news spread quietly.

As Hart ducked under a spray of hot water, the club steward checked out the evidence: a heap of worn-out clothing, pointy-toed cowboy boots and a coat that smelled like a dying dog. For a minute he thought some tramp had eluded his watch. They'd tried it before. When the water stopped, he ducked out of sight, waited till the stealthy one had dressed and disappeared, then made a beeline exit for the bar, pretending not to notice Hart, who had slumped in a leather lounge chair, and taken the phone on his lap. He was back in his office just in time to close the door and pick up the extension.

Sandrine's phone rang three times before the answering machine kicked in. The perfumed trill of her telephone voice took Hart by surprise. Her message began in flirtatious French, soon switching to English in a lower pitch. Her French was a boarding school variety that reminded Hart of small, delicate flowers. Her English was brisk, in fact, brisk was her normal rhythm, unless the occasion specifically called for something else.

As the message came to an end, he said nothing, held the phone stiff until finally the tape ran out and the dial tone cut in.

Then he hung up, and called back again, unsure of what he'd just heard.

Bonjour, vous avez . . . You have reached the answering machine of Sandrine Lamotte. Please leave a message . . . If you're calling regarding the Hart Granger Memorial, you may leave a message, or simply join us in the ballroom of the McGill Faculty Club, 3450 McTavish Street. The event begins at five p.m. (Then, with an ever-so-slight falter in her voice,) *Thank you. Merci.*

When he was sure Hart had left the building, the club steward made a quick perusal of the membership. They'd all been invited – he'd tacked a personal letter from Sandrine on the notice board three weeks ago. He considered his Christmas tips. He asked himself who would most appreciate insider advice on the absolute necessity of attending Hart Granger's memorial?

EIGHT

A diminutive mock-Tudor edifice sitting like an abandoned toy amid a dense grove of steely glass office towers, the Racket Club had always made Hart think of *Alice in Wonderland*. Never more so than the morning he leapt out into the street after a surreptitious shower like a twitchy rabbit pursued by opium dreams.

All winter, he'd been careful to remain incommunicado with the past. From time to time he wondered how they were dealing with his disappearance, half expecting someone, Vince or Amanda if not Sandrine, to track him down and pass raw judgement on his mission. He assumed his old life was standing still, that upon his return it would need to be kick-started or resisted, depending on who said what in the first few hours.

The farthest his imagination had gone was a leisurely lunch with Sandrine during which he would naturally be forced to account for his time away. He was rehearsing a succinct, fairly truthful account of "a friend's death" which he hoped would prompt a minimum of questions. The juxtaposition of René's baroque world with Sandrine's inquisitive mind would not work at all.

So he was formally 'dead,' in Montreal? The idea lightened his mood considerably. What better way to start a new life?

The end of irony? Apparently not.

Walking by the plate-glass windows of The Bay, he caught a reflection of himself, and stopped. Picturing the ballroom full of Sandrine's choice of friends, all of whom expected him to be dead, he laughed.

A woman approaching from a distance heard. Catching sight of him, she shrieked, covered her mouth with her hands. Then she picked up speed, and cutting a wide swath between them, veered to the edge of the sidewalk and hurried past. He did not catch her eye, but as soon as she'd gone by, he realised she looked familiar. Turning around, he saw her walking briskly toward Place des Arts. He thought he recognised the actress, his neighbour from the Venice beach house. For a moment, he was tempted to run after her.

Turning up the hill, he studied the pavement as he walked, pursuing the woman's reaction to its dull conclusion. What was she doing in Montreal? Was she here for the memorial? Why did she run off?

Recalling Sandrine's voice on the message machine, he noted a thread of efficiency woven through gravity. He began to see beyond the theoretical irony of his sudden appearance. Spontaneity was not Sandrine's strong point. She expected life to go according to her plan.

Why come back now, to face a chorus of the past? The idea induced a sudden flash of dread. May be time to run, he thought. How often does the opportunity come along? He could step back on the train and head further east, where a new identity would be his for the making. Get out while it was still possible.

On the other hand, eventually they were bound to find out he was still alive. He could not hope to remain incognito forever. As he turned onto Sherbrooke Street, he wondered who'd made it onto the invitation list. Then he remembered hearing the word 'ballroom.' He'd attended few wedding receptions in the ballroom, a sunken Edwardian fantasy built in the 1930s. Whatever possessed Sandrine to choose the

Faculty Club, an academic institution? Any number of down-town bars would have been infinitely better. If it had been his choice. But wasn't contempt for Sandrine's decision a form of snobbery? *It's a memorial, for Christ's sake! A gesture from a woman who believes you're dead! NB: learn to love humanity.* The voice of reason began to nag.

He looked up. He was standing in front of Holt's. A bum holding out an empty coffee cup opened the door, so he went inside.

Holt Renfrew may not be the most prestigious department store in Montreal, but the management works hard at projecting that impression. When visiting film stars ask their people where to purchase impressive name-brand souvenirs, Holt's is on the list, which is why the high-cheek-boned beauty behind the perfume counter flashed her ten-thousand dollar smile in Hart's direction, because two weeks earlier, a similarly attired "bum" had spent half an hour talking about himself, then laid down $500 U.S. for three bottles of her favourite scent.

Hart responded favourably to the beauty counsellor's fluttering *bonjour*. He was happy to chat in French. Co-incidentally, the young lady was selling Lancôme. Her personal favourite was *Trésor,* which also happened to be Sandrine's.

"Is it a special occasion, *monsieur*?" she cooed.

"Yes, my funeral," he said, unsmiling. She giggled, then asked whether he wanted the box gift wrapped. He handed over his American Express card and said thanks. He'd be in the men's department, selecting a suit for the occasion.

Under normal circumstances, Hart would have known exactly what he wanted and wasted no time making a decision. Augostino, the clerk who approached him, was a natty Italian in his sixties. He took one look at the Stetson buckskin ensemble, the long grey hair, and decided his customer was a true eccentric, no doubt rich and in need of severe guidance. Aware conversation would complicate things, Hart said only that he had a reception to attend later in the day, so any alterations would have to be done immediately.

Augostino's choices ran to a single-button leather jacket, or, if that was too heavy, a box cut with brass buttons from Canali, in a savoury burnt orange linen. Either would look great over an off-white Armani silk shirt with a Chinese collar, top button left undone. He suggested a medium-weight linen weave pant, preferably cream.

Hart favoured dark blue or grey for business. He wore brown once, but it didn't feel right. Now he was being asked to choose from a completely different end of Holt's stock, and three sizes below what he normally wore. The linen pants fit perfectly. They looked all right with the orange jacket. He glanced down at the tag: the jacket alone was priced at $1,350. He handed over his VISA.

Augostino was elated. "*Magnifique, monsieur.* It is not many men who can get away with this look but I believe you can do it!"

The pants needed hemming. Agostino assured him this was no problem, the seamstress would get to work immediately.

Hart was beginning to sniff a potentially ghoulish side to this rendezvous with the past. The circumstances were unpredictable, to say the least. He tied his hair back and practiced a smile, thinking that a sense of humour was essential to what lay ahead. Humour, and great presentation. The total bounced up on the cash register screen. He shuddered, but said nothing. Regardless of the cost, he knew it was not a good idea to show up at the Faculty Club looking dead.

Still, he'd worn the same clothes for months – an innocuous rotation of faded jeans and t-shirts. He was uneasy outside the familiar loose fit of old skin. He tried to see himself walking into one of Sandrine's events, this one celebrating his life and death. The picture was a sombre haze. The back of his neck prickled. Sweat beads formed on his brow.

"I'm sorry, sir . . . Sir?" Augostino was holding out the credit card.

Hart snapped out of his reverie. Something was wrong. "Pardon?"

"I am afraid this card doesn't work," Augostino said. The tone was polite but his lips curled. Hart opened his wallet, looking for an alternative. He remembered he'd given it to the perfume lady.

"Hold on," he said. "I've left the other card out front." The perfume clerk was waiting for him. There was no sign of a gift-wrapped box in sight. Both credit cards had been cancelled. He mumbled something about finding a bank machine, and fled.

When he stepped out into the street, the bum was waiting. He shook the few coins in the bottom of his paper cup and smirked. The man's scorn cut deep. Hart slipped his hand inside his jacket. The folded notebook was still there. When he'd put a few blocks between himself and the bum, he took it out and scribbled, "Must avoid returning to old life. Abjure superficial judgements. Do not let greed-ego-other people into the space created by all that has happened."

The words were faint, hardly legible. Walking on, he thought, everybody needs to eat, sleep in warmth and feel free to move ahead, or not. These are human essentials. Pets deserve them too. But the whole edifice of judgement, the scramble to get a leg up – it made him queasy.

NINE

The first warm sunny day after a Montreal winter calls forth a burst of good cheer. If not the true beginning of spring, the day of Hart's memorial was at least a promising taste, so that people who skipped up the Faculty Club's stone steps late in the afternoon needed a gust of Mozart to deliver them unto solemnity.

A hundred and fifty-odd people filled the ornate sunken ballroom with a whir of grave excitement. As Sandrine took her place on a raised dais at the far end of the room, the string quartet caught her nod and faded their Requiem on a resolute note. She was wearing a trim twill suit, lime green. Beside her, on a sturdy rostrum, was a metal box the size of a small accordion – Hart's ashes, which she had only recently succeeded in bringing home from L.A. There were no chairs, only a few small tables scattered along the walls, covered with linen clothes and set with bouquets of white roses. Attractive young men in svelte pants and tuxedo shirts circulated with glasses of wine on trays.

At twenty minutes after five, those who had a formal part to play in the proceedings made their way toward the podium. Vince stood next to Sandrine, Tom on one side of Amanda, Neil on the other. Lenny had secured a place in the front row, where he could offer Sandrine maximum eye contact.

She carried a cotton handkerchief. Her hands trembled as she placed her cue cards on the lectern. She looked down at the printed words, the highlighted phrases, then back at the assembled. As she stepped forward, the room's attention turned her way. The microphone caught a sharp intake of breath. "At times like this," she began, her voice trailing off. She looked down at her notes, started over.

"At times like this we gather . . . to be together in . . . in . . . (an inaudible whisper). To remember . . . someone we . . . have . . . loved." Pausing, she began re-arranging the order of the cards as though she'd misplaced something important, then, shoulders shaking, turned away. The mourners were still. The waiters stopped pouring. Lenny sensed a dark cloud moving over a bright day.

Amanda caught Tom's eye, and gave him a meaningful nod. He moved over, put a hand on Sandrine's shoulder and whispered, "It's all right. Let me start off. You can come in later." She nodded and ceded her position in front of the microphone.

Since his conversation with Amanda on the way into Montreal, Tom had been compiling mental notes for a pos-sible tribute to his late brother-in-law, should the occasion arise. Thinking of Hart brought to mind a few good stories, and helped pass the time while Neil and Amanda made watery conversation out of nothing. Since the news of Hart's death was months old, he'd envisioned more of a roast than a funeral. Facing the crowd now, he saw that Sandrine's stum-ble had plunged the room into tender sympathy. An accom-plished trial lawyer, he knew better than to pit himself against the jury's mood.

"Hart Granger," he began, in his best Boston Irish cathe-dral voice, "was a man we shall not soon forget." As if on cue, the crowd broke into applause. The impromptu eulogy that followed drew on familiar phrases gleaned from a life-time of funeral going, his intention being to stall for time until Sandrine and other members of the inner circle had summoned the courage to take over. Careful not to steal their thunder, he launched into to a general discussion of death, how it inevitably catches us off guard, returns us to the ever-pressing issue of mortality. Heads nodded. The maître d' gave a sign and the waiters resumed discreetly topping up empty glasses.

As he talked, the room's anxiety melted. He made favourable references to Sandrine, who by now had recovered and was ready to take the floor. Tom left no point of entry in his masterful summation. He covered the philosophical bases thoroughly. Finally, after squeezing a faint chuckle from the crowd, he decided to risk one of his Hart anecdotes – a favourite, in case there wasn't time for more.

"Looking out on the crowd today, I see stalwarts from the Montreal Racket Club. Hart was a member. A member in good standing? I don't know. I'd say hockey was Hart's game. For twenty consecutive winters, he laced up to play on the outdoor rinks of Verdun. Several of his teammates are here, Ti'Jean, Jimmy J., Pete the Hulk O'Bourne, Rocket the Menace. Am I missing anybody? Well the hockey team will remember, I'm sure, a fishing trip they took together in the Laurentians. The fish survived, but unfortunately the lodge burned down."

Hart's hockey cronies laughed heartily, and a few around them caught the mood. But an equal force of cold anger emanated from Racket Club VP Arthur Madden, the owner of said fishing lodge, which had been in the family for generations and was worth close to half a million dollars. Hart had claimed he wanted to entertain a new woman in style and Madden liked the idea of providing lovers with a getaway.

Madden had been out of the country at the time. He'd more or less accepted the unfortunate fire as bad luck, until now. Tom pinned it firmly on the hockey bums who were standing right beside him.

The punch line was a clever remark from Hart. The audience laughed, but Madden didn't catch it. He was straining to hear Ti'Jean and Rocket the Menace as they went over the lurid details of that fateful weekend. they knew it was Madden's cottage they'd wrecked by drunkenly leaving embers in the campfire when they all went off for a midnight dip. A spark had leapt onto a pile of newspapers. They spotted the flames from the middle of the lake. By the time they got to shore, it was too late. The main building was engulfed.

While they laughed, Madden smouldered.

"I guess the English pig was pretty well insured," he heard Ti'Jean say, in French.

As the waiter passed in front of him, Madden took two glasses, downed one and gripped the other. Looking around the room, he caught the eyes of two old boys from the Racket Club. They shared his opinion. Then he saw the club steward, smiling helplessly.

Audience approval galvanized the speaker. Having established a comic tone, Tom continued his impromptu Life and Times of Hart Granger for seventeen minutes (Sandrine was counting), during which time virtually everyone in the room got a piece of information he or she had not possessed while the departed walked among them. She rocked back on her heels. Lenny saw the fire rising in her eyes, grief giving way to anger.

Determined to appear magnanimous, Sandrine had invited most of the women Hart had dated since their divorce.

When Tom told a story about the time he had accompanied Hart as he cruised transvestite bars in the Village, he hastened to quash suspicion of the deceased's sexual orientation by stressing that at the end of the night, Hart had gone off with a 'real woman.' Had he not made a point of identifying the year and month, the two women Hart had been dating at the time might not have taken such offence. Sandrine, though not exactly jealous, was furious.

For a good part of his eulogy, Tom's wit, his boyish good looks and immaculate sense of timing held the crowd, but as the arrows of revelation penetrated all corners, Amanda began to sense discomfort. She tried to catch Tom's eye, but the Irish raconteur in full flight was unstoppable.

Sandrine held her breath, ready to give him fifteen seconds more. Just as she was about to step in, Tom launched into one of his favourite Irish wake jokes and the hall burst into thunderous laughter, a gush of nerves leading to applause. The ovation provided a temporary restraint on those who would by then have paid serious money to see the dead man throttled.

Before Sandrine could move, Tom handed the microphone over to Amanda.

TEN

Hart entered the antechamber leading to the ballroom just after Tom had revealed the truth about Madden's cottage. The sound of laughter, followed by applause, came as a relief. He had circled the building four times, started up the stairs, turned back twice. Finally, curiosity triumphed over a gut-deep feeling that his unannounced arrival could go terribly wrong. Tom's effect on the crowd was reassuring. He could see himself walking right in and making everybody laugh. It was only a matter of choosing the right moment.

A lavish buffet covered three huge tables in the anteroom, ready for guests after the speeches. Normally, the sight of a smorgasbord would have killed his appetite, so thoroughly had months of deprivation warped his taste buds. But this artful array of finger foods looked tempting. He helped himself to a shrimp with Cajun dip. When a waiter paused with a tray of red wine in crystal glasses (rented, the Faculty Club had nothing in Sandrine's league), he took one, and savoured the rich bouquet. As Amanda's clear, girlish voice rolled over him, as sweet and tingly as an innocent encounter with the *Wizard of Oz*, he tried a crab ball, followed by a bread stick dipped in garlic tapenade.

"I have to admit," she began, "there was a time when I doubted Hart was really dead. I mean, I just couldn't believe . . . I'm sure some of you will understand. A guy like him, slipping away, on the phone. I just – well, I thought there must be some mistake. But no, that was *me*. My *desire* to deny. He's definitely here with us today (she glanced at the accordion box of ashes on the stand beside her). Hart is with us, I know. So I want to be the one to say how glad we are – (she looked lovingly down at Neil who stood with hands folded, head bowed solemnly) – as a family, we are so glad to see so many of Hart's friends turn out to remember him, and we hope you all have a good time. (Laughter) I don't mean a *good time*. Well, yes, I do. Hart would want people to come together and have a party."

She was giddy with nerves. The mood was contagious. Hart licked the caviar from a thumb-sized medallion of pumpernickel, and crammed two devilled egg halves into his mouth.

"My husband Tom told a few stories that, if I'd known about them before hand, would not necessarily have been told. (Laughs) He's a lawyer, what more can I say? All right, so Tom's forgiven? Then I, too, would like to relate something about Hart that you don't know. Maybe this is more than remembering Hart. Maybe this is all about getting to know him. Sometimes I wonder . . . I wonder if we can ever know another person? Let's leave that to philosophers (nod to Sandrine). Instead, I'll tell you a story about Hart that pretty well sums him up. At least I think it does.

"When I was five years old, I was a timid little girl with no courage and no imagination. I was in awe of my brother. He was tall and smart and . . . sometimes he could seem almost, well, wicked. By that I mean he had all the sterling qualities necessary for success in this mean old world, and I had none of them. Then one night, Hart came into my room. He sat on my bed, and he told me a secret. He said we'd had an older brother named Bill, but Mum and Dad got rid of Bill so there would be room for me."

The room fell silent. The waiters paused to listen. Hart downed another four spicy shrimps, and helped himself to a second glass of Château Lafitte.

"I cannot overstate how much stress this story caused me. I've been in therapy about it. I've even written a piece that was published in a magazine. Finally, I got around to understanding, forgiving, thanking Hart for his meanness. Because what he said was *true*. There *was* an older brother. His name is Neil." She beamed a smile in Neil's direction.

"He's a fantastic older brother, and he's part of our family now, although at the time that Hart guessed our family secret, Neil was still making his way in the world. Playing professional hockey, things like that. Weren't you Neil? Come on, don't be so modest. Neil is a very modest guy." She blew Neil a kiss.

"All right, what do I want to say about my middle brother, Hart? He was . . . sometimes mean . . . but most of the time, protective. He could be selfish, or give you everything. He was aggressive, and he was cool. He was funny. Clever. Most of all, he had a great capacity to live the moment, without all those anxieties that make the rest of us trudge along through one commonplace duty after another.

"Once, I overheard our parents talking, and they said he was a genius. I believed them. I still do. Hart was a genius. Genius doesn't necessary mean the person is going to make some major, memorable contribution to humanity. If Dad were alive, I'd tell him that, because he passed away thinking Hart was a failure. At least, a disappointment. I would tell our father that Hart's *life* was his work of genius.

"I don't quite know how to put into words what my dear, dear brother meant to me. I hope somehow – can't say

I believe, but yes, I hope there is an afterlife, for my own sake. 'Cause I really cannot bear the thoughts that Hart is . . . nothing but . . . a pile of ashes, sitting here in this box. I hope somehow Hart can *hear* what I've got to say about him. There was so much I wanted to say. And I didn't get to say it . . ."

As Amanda's voice faltered, Hart finished the last of five chocolate-coated strawberries. Sure that his moment was at hand, he peeked around the corner of the doorframe and caught sight of his sister, dressed in black. She looked at the ceiling as she spoke.

"Wherever you are, William Hartford Granger, hear this: I didn't always appreciate your . . . sensibility. But your existence made my life bigger and bolder and better than I could have made it myself. I miss you. I love you. I thank you. Good-bye." The audience responded with applause. A lump rose in Hart's throat, followed by a hiccup.

Sandrine twisted her gold bracelet until it began to irritate her wrist. Seizing the microphone, she raised it to her level. The amp let out a wild screech, which brought the soundman to her side. Those near the speakers began to smell a faint aroma of smoke, but the technician was too busy with Sandrine's volume problem to notice.

"I was married to Hart once," she began, to nervous laughter. "Amanda—" the system let out a sharp whine. After a few seconds delay, she saw the technician nod, and began again.

"Amanda, don't take it personally, dear. He was mean to me too. (Cathartic laughter from those who were whipped into anger by Tom.) But he was also sweet. I learned a lot about marriage from Hart. About negative capability. Endurance. Patience. Crisis management. (She glanced at Lenny, who grinned with embarrassment.)

"Hart's passing was a shock. As I'm sure many of you will agree, it is only with distance, after a winter without him, that we can begin to appreciate his . . . his . . . contribution. It's true those closest to him often felt we didn't know Hart. And it turns out we were right. We could not have known, when he was alive, how generous and thoughtful he was, how incredibly organised. Who could have imagined that a man who routinely lost his dry cleaning slips, never rotated his tires, rarely recycled – that such an individual would have crafted an enduring legacy?

"Friends, colleagues, next of kin, we come here not to bury Hart Granger, but to remember him. His sister has spoken at length about Hart's private, human qualities. I would like to speak about his public legacy. Because Hart Granger did care very much about the echo his life would have throughout eternity. To some extent credit must go to his perspicacious lawyer, (nod to the back row) Jack McDougall, who advised Hart to forge such an imaginative testament. I am inclined to believe that Hart had a premonition he would not live to be old. He was prepared to leave us."

She paused long enough to let the idea settle.

"Hart Granger was a surprising man. Those of us who have benefited from his legacy – Vince, Hart's partner – he'll be speaking for himself in a moment – Vince and I have combined our efforts to ensure that Hart's legacy will endure. We have created the Hart Granger Scholarship at McGill University. Five thousand dollars each year, to be awarded to the PhD student whose proposed research most closely resembles values espoused by the man we have gathered here to honour. Those values have been articulated in an essay prepared by Vince and myself." She waited for applause; the audience obeyed.

"The foundation will be administered through the Institute for Advanced Creative Dynamics, of which I am the founder and director, here at McGill University. All further donations will benefit from a full tax receipt. The details are spelled out in our brochure, which the waiters will be passing around shortly."

Emboldened by more wine than he'd consumed in months, Hart stepped incautiously through the doorway to see whether it was Sandrine speaking, or some fetid hallucination arising from the gases of too much finger food. The trepidation that had gripped him through Amanda's testimony disappeared. The idea of his money funding Sandrine's self-promoting Institute for Fellow Flakes made him furious.

Suspicious already that the gorging latecomer might not be an invited guest, the maître d' noticed Hart's agitation, and laid a hand on his arm. "Excuse me, sir," he said, firm but calm.

Hart brushed him off and ploughed into the crowd. The first person to recognise him was Wanda. Lulled by medication, she was vulnerable to shock, and at the sight of a dead man stalking, let fly a cinematic scream. Whereupon events overtook all expectations Hart had had of his resurrection.

Wanda's scream startled Neil, who lunged backwards into the podium and knocked the metal box of ashes flying. The smouldering amp blew up, causing a thunderous explosion. Someone shouted, "Bomb!"

Tutored by the terrible times in which they lived, people dove for the floor, others made for the door. Screams magnified shouts, creating hysteria. Within seconds, the coincidental outburst of calamities unleashed the roar of pandemonium on the ballroom.

Tom was the first to realise what had happened. He caught the technician's frantic waving of arms. The metal box had bounced against the amp, adding to the noise but surviving the fall intact. While the technician scrambled to unhook the fried equipment, Tom tried to get the room's attention, and failed.

Lenny was the first person Hart faced among the many who stormed past him, frantic to reach the exit. Hart knew who he was in an instant. He was the only person in the room Hart did not recognise. Furthermore, he was wearing an expensive suit and a pretentious haircut – exactly the kind of man Sandrine would go for if he stepped out of sight. Whether carnal instinct played a part in Hart's response to falling upon a rival would be impossible to prove. Surely other factors contributed to what happened. The accumulation of rich food swallowed quickly and the jolt of so many staring faces made him dizzy. The explosion, the screams, were profoundly disorienting. He had never been completely at ease with his decision to attend his own memorial. On the positive side: ego, curiosity, and a wicked sense of humour, so lovingly noted and forgiven by his sister in her eulogy, which had brought tears to his eyes. Still, at the last minute, he'd been prey to tender feelings more recently acquired, to fear, anxiety, a deep desire not to disturb or unsettle other people, or to be unsettled himself. He had grown older since his friends last saw him. Wiser, a little fragile. Just this morning, his freshly tenderised psyche had received a deluge of bad news about the state of the world. He carried the clippings in his pocket. The world, the shrimp, the eulogies. And now Lenny.

The room spun around him. From somewhere in the blur, he heard a peel of laughter, and leaned forward, desperate to escape. But his feet wouldn't move. The too-quick mix of party edibles gathered strength. Determined to fight the next wave, he took a step, but movement set off a charge. The unhappy cargo exploded, sending a gale force spray of vomit straight at the lone figure who blocked his path.

The first blow stunned Lenny. It hit him in the crotch. As he leaned over in disbelief to look, a second outburst flew into his hair, splattering his shirt and jacket.

Weakened by the sudden loss of too much food so recently swallowed, Hart swayed. The room's attention had been diverted his way. He caught a panorama of shocked faces, people he had known forever. Arthur Madden, surrounded by Hart's hockey buddies, furious. Vince, a sheepish shade of white. Amanda, making her way toward him, cheeks glowing, her arms reaching out.

He teetered gratefully in her direction, but before they could embrace, Sandrine stepped in. A fierce paragon in lime, she blocked Amanda's path. Hart opened his mouth to speak and took a sharp whack on the right cheek. His black Stetson, which he had been too timid to remove, flew into the crowd. He reeled back in pain.

"How could you?" Sandrine shouted. "How could you do this to me!?"

She flung her arm back as if to strike him again, but a nearby scuffle diverted her attention. Emboldened by the sight of a woman taking action, Madden punched Ti'Jean hard in the stomach. Rocket the Menace slugged Madden in the chin, and two other players stepped in to prevent a full-scale brawl. In the distance, Tom's voice rose about the fracas, begging everyone to calm down.

Hart sank to his knees. Everything went black.

As he lay crumpled on the floor, vaguely aware of distant voices, faces flashed through his mind. The very people he'd been eager to forget were all present, a bitter reminder of the fiftieth, when he'd known Sandrine was planning something. She'd dropped a dozen hints. Still, the sight of fifty people shouting surprise had turned his spirit foul. Only copious amounts of liquor had got him through. Crowds were not the kind of attention he enjoyed, and this was a thousand times worse.

He had fallen on his right arm. Lucidity returned with a vengeance. He felt the pain but was afraid to move, or give any sign of life. Pinned down by monstrous foreboding, he thought in stark terms: life – no/death – fine! But how to will death? If will dies, does the body follow? He murmured: die, die, die.

Suddenly, he felt his body levitate, as if a crane had picked him up from the depths. Hot breath on his neck, the smell of another man. Opening his eyes, he saw he was less than six inches away from a big, sloppy grin. Neil had hoisted him out of the pool of puke, and was carrying him, like a defeated mouse, through the crowd.

"'Scuse me, 'scuse me," Neil kept saying over and over, as if people weren't already shrinking back from the sight of a stinking corpse being lugged away. The last thing Hart heard before he and his big brother disappeared into the men's room was the sound of Camelot-cool Tom testing the emergency microphone with a message to the survivors.

"Ladies and gentlemen, could I have your attention, please. All right, everything's fine now. Absolutely nothing to worry about. A series of unfortunate incidents. Question and answer period is coming right up. In the meantime, Sandrine invites everyone to an outstanding buffet, accompanied by some truly magnificent wines. Please stay and, ah, celebrate with us. Dear friends . . . as they say, the Lord works in strange and mysterious ways."

Sandrine never did find out who gave orders to the string quartet. The lead insisted later he had been following instructions, though his description of the man who gave the nod was so vague that no one could figure out who it had been. But just as the inner circle of mourners learned that nothing awful had happened, the quartet struck up a lively rendition of "Sentimental Journey." A few seconds later, the ubiquitous Leroy Hotlips Munger joined in on his saxophone. For years to come, those present would recall the occasion as one of the most musically satisfying times of their lives.

ELEVEN

Word soon spread through the crowd that Hart's death had been nothing more than a rumour, the memorial, some kind of performance art piece, possibly an experiment designed by the Institute for Advanced Creative Dynamics. All theories gained credibility from the sudden transformation of a solemn string quartet into an upbeat jazz quintet. Furthermore, the wine was, as Tom had promised, outstanding. Half an hour after Hart's swoon, the hundred-odd people who remained were crammed into the unspoiled antechamber, talking and laughing freely.

Sandrine had drawn up her guest list with an eye to promoting the scholarship foundation, so there were more than a few present who had no direct acquaintanceship with the deceased – business people, journalists, organisation-minded academics, professional net-workers. Off-putting though it had been at the time, Hart's heave-ho and the simultaneous clap of electrical thunder turned out to be an effective ice-breaker. The atmosphere crackled with the expectation that he would reappear any minute and explain his existence.

Lenny was sponging puke off his pants when Neil and Hart burst through the washroom door. He apologised profusely for getting in the way, and fled. He found Sandrine in the Heritage Room, a salon adjoining the ballroom where the catering staff accessed the supply of liquor and extra food. From a distance he saw she was gripping the maître d's arm, shoulders shaking, and assumed she must be distraught. As he drew closer, he realised she was giving orders. Strictly speaking, only waiters were allowed to touch liquor but Sandrine insisted every man-jack in black pants pitch in and get the wine flowing.

"Sandrine," he whispered, trying to take her hand.

"Just a minute, Lenny. Olivier, you listen to me. I don't care if you have to do it yourself. The next fifteen minutes are crucial. You've got to be sure everyone gets a glass of wine, or they'll leave. And by the way, I thought we were serving shrimp?"

A portly gent, Olivier had turned red with consternation. He hated deviations from the plan as much as he hated taking orders. "We had two trays. Someone nibbled during the speeches."

"Nobody in the ballroom was eating shrimp," she snapped. "I was there."

Lenny tugged at her sleeve, "Let's go."

She laughed. "Darling! I can't leave now. There are hundreds of people here."

"Hart's not dead," he muttered grimly, as thought the day had been ruined.

"I know! Isn't it wonderful? I can hardly wait to hear what he has to say for himself."

"But you hit him. Aren't you furious? What an asshole!"

"Leonard, he's *alive*. Doesn't that mean anything to you?"

"Sandreeeeeene."

Sandrine hated whining. It was one of Leonard's few faults. He understood that most social events were elaborately disguised professional engagements, but he was prone to peevishness when her attention stayed too long on other people. She tried to be patient, hoping he would outgrow possessiveness.

"Get yourself a glass of wine, dear. Mingle. We are not leaving this function." She squeezed his forearm affectionately, and slipped away. He shrugged, and strode toward the door.

Amanda was eager to see Hart and tried to follow him into the men's room, but Tom insisted she stay back. "He needs a little time, honey. He'll be out when he's ready."

"But where has he been all these months?" she moaned.

"That's something only Hart can answer."

It was Tom who put the Do Not Disturb sign on the men's room door after he peeked in and saw Neil and Hart sitting on the floor like schoolboys, smoking. Hart sat cross-legged; Neil was leaning up against a wall. A sweet, laconic aroma filled the air. When they saw Tom, conversation stopped.

"We need a few minutes, here," Neil said authoritatively. So, he brought them a couple of bottles of water, and tacked a sign on the door.

As the few minutes stretched into an hour, Tom realised that promising the startled mourners a Q & A session might have been a bit rash. With the mocking tone of a roast, the eulogies had done more to arouse interest in the unknown Hart than to put a dead man to rest. Now that he was alive and present, people wanted more. But Hart and Neil were obviously in no rush to face the crowd. Tom wondered just how long the guests would wait.

In fact, they stayed until the wine ran out, then drifted toward the door. Amanda and Sandrine presided over the goodbyes, assuring everyone who asked they had no idea where Hart had been for the past seven months, or indeed whose ashes languished on the podium. Those who left business cards and email addresses were promised answers as soon as the situation became clear.

As the last mourner disappeared, Sandrine gave Olivier a hug. Amanda and Tom sat down to wait on a brocade sofa in the foyer.

Finally, Neil stuck his head out the men's room door. Finding no one in sight, he motioned to Hart, who followed. Amanda saw them first, and ran over to Hart, threw her arms around his bony frame and burst into tears.

By the looks on their faces – Neil's grin tinged with excitement, Hart's ironic smirk – she figured Neil knew everything and Hart was unlikely to say more, at least not for the moment. She didn't mind, she could wait for the details. The miracle of Hart's return cast a beatific glow. Her public confession over his (supposed) ashes had been a great relief. Knowing he'd not only heard but was alive and therefore able to make amends, she was sure there would never be another cloudy day in paradise. From now on everyone would be together for Christmas.

Sandrine saw the four of them standing in a huddle and strode across the room, arms stretched out to receive Hart. He allowed himself to be hugged. Standing stiff as a kayak, he turned his head sideways to miss her lips.

"You're thin!" she cried. "You look fabulous."

Even Neil, who had seen the old Hart all of twice, had trouble grasping what she meant. He guessed from Tom's muffled snort that he wasn't alone in his doubts. Sandrine chose to ignore the intervention.

"Well, this is quite a turn of events," she said, breathlessly. "You are a man of surprises, Hart. So, shall we all go out to dinner?" She spoke as though she'd been nursing the plan for weeks.

Hart glared. "Get the ashes," he said to Neil, who nodded, and disappeared into the ballroom.

"Are you all right?" Tom asked. Hart knew the question was rhetorical; the next move was his.

"I'm not hungry," he said.

Sandrine pressed on, "Oh, Hart. You must be. When you look at a menu . . ."

"No," he said, flatly. "I need sleep."

Suddenly offended, she raised herself to the limit of her stilettos. "Well then, would you mind telling me what's going on? I knocked myself out for this memorial, on the assumption you were dead. I think I deserve an explanation."

"Sorry to disappoint you."

Tom and Amanda recognised the beginning of a long night. They knew from experience that neither Hart nor Sandrine could resist their favourite cocktail made from indignation, accusation, and a twist of sarcasm. Once they got started, all present would be called upon to take sides.

Hart squared his shoulders in preparation for a serious offensive. "About my money—"

"Surely this is not about money!" Sandrine seethed.

For years to come, Hart would abjure spicy shrimp, turn away from the sight of crab balls and tapenade, spurn cream puffs and strawberries. Similarly, the idea of caviar on pumpernickel would make his stomach clench. The delicacies that had done him in were a Pavlovian inoculation against smorgasbords in general, and hors d'oeurve of any kind. He'd have no choice but to resist. Similarly, watching

Sandrine glower over him, he took note of her lime suit, the chiselled coiffure, strong sensuous lips that formed so easily around caustic accusation. Whether love had or did still exist was suddenly irrelevant. In that moment, he lost his taste for the old order. She was fiery; he needed gentle. He knew it was a matter of life or death.

As for Sandrine, although she'd said he looked great, she'd been nervous, and determined to say the right thing. In truth, she thought he'd grown carelessly thin. Weight loss brought nothing of the usual glow that comes from self-denial. Stripped of the extra pounds, he was short, power-less. After months beside tallish Leonard Rosenthal, she had lost the habit of looking down. Furthermore, she consid-ered Hart's attire a personal affront. Obviously, he'd planned to crash the memorial, and made an effort to embarrass her by dressing inappropriately. Selfishness aside, she decided his aging-rebel look lacked authenticity.

All of this Sandrine could have told him, unflinching, in the presence of his next of kin. But she did not. Nor did Hart venture to speak his mind. Twitches of love and hate stirred amid the debris of unanswered questions, but neither of them felt the urge to jump. It was that simple. While Tom and Amanda looked on, unsuspecting best man and maid of honour, the friendly divorce dissolved.

Of course, they didn't know it at the time. Fearing fur-ther eruption, Amanda glanced at Tom, pleading for help. He tried to take charge. "All right, I think we all need to just go somewhere and . . ."

Before he could finish, Neil reappeared with the box of ashes. Hart bristled, expecting interrogation. Amanda turned to Neil and asked, "What happened to Wanda?"

Looking vaguely guilty, Neil mumbled, "I guess she must have gone back to the hotel." He shifted the box against his chest, as if it were precious cargo.

"Then we have to get back and find her," Amanda said, taking Hart by the arm. "Sandrine, you've done a wonderful job with . . . this. Really, outstanding. Why don't we just call each other, tomorrow? Tom, let's go. I think we should check on Wanda, and then, Hart – Hart you must be exhausted."

Taking his cue, Tom jumped in and kissed Sandrine on both cheeks. Neil followed suit, uneasy with the show of public affection but eager to learn. As they started for the door, Olivier beckoned Sandrine to join him in the Heritage Room, where they would settle the fate of leftovers. She reached Lenny on her cell phone. He agreed to swing by and pick her up.

TWELVE

In the fall of 1965, Terrance Granger was appointed head of the cardio unit, his first serious promotion at the Montreal General Hospital. He celebrated by taking Kitty to Chez La Mère Michel, a new gourmet restaurant on Guy Street, below Ste-Catherine. The prices were astronomical but the food was outstanding. Kitty experienced something of an epiphany that night. In the candlelight of table number eight, she was swept up in her husband's optimism, and for the first time in their marriage, let herself relax into good fortune.

Terrance was determined to make his mark in medicine. He took the promotion as nothing less than what he deserved, a step on the way to Chief of Surgery. She wished she had his confidence. Most days she felt terribly undeserving. Two lovely children and a handsome, successful husband – the present seemed unreal. She sometimes caught herself floating, as though she were playing a role onstage. Any minute the scene might stop and a voice from the back row cry out, "Aren't you the girl who . . . ?"

Finally, in a fancy French restaurant, in this most unreal moment, she had her first glimpse beyond the vertiginous present. It happened when he said, "This is *our* restaurant. We're going to come here when I get Hanover's job, so let's hope Chez La Mère stays in business for a while." He used his best, commanding tone, the one that terrified underlings and turned the children quiet, and she believed him. Sure enough, a few celebratory dinners later, Terrance got what he knew he deserved.

After their father died, Hart and Amanda always took Kitty to La Mère Michel on her birthday. That they came to choose that particular restaurant after the drama of Hart's memorial would in future seem eerily just. But in the chaos of the moment, it was quite accidental.

They arrived back at the hotel to find Wanda asleep with the bedroom door shut. Neil went in to check on her. She was face down, her head twisted at an odd angle. He moved her into a more comfortable position and covered her with the spare blanket. He smelled liquor on her breath, suspected it was a chaser to prescription drugs. He combed his hair, brushed his teeth, and told the others she was fighting a flu bug.

"She'll be fine tomorrow," he said.

All attention focused on Hart, who looked like he might bolt at any minute. He turned down Amanda's plan to start with a cup of tea and order up food from a nearby take-out, said he couldn't stay. He complained about the hotel suite's lack of ventilation. When Tom suggested they get some air and have a smoked meat sandwich at a deli near the hotel, Hart did not object. Amanda wanted to wake up Wanda, but Neil insisted she'd be better off with a good night's sleep.

On the way down in the elevator, Hart said he wasn't keen on Ben's. "I've been off meat for a while."

Since it was his first reference to the seven months during which he'd been presumed dead, everyone took him seriously. There was talk about a Greek seafood place on Park Avenue, but Hart winced mysteriously. Finally, as they got into a taxi, Amanda thought of La Mère Michel. She was delighted when Hart shrugged acceptance. A full-scale French restaurant meant they'd have at least two hours of serious contact. There was no chance he could avoid the obvious subject at such close range.

As they sped along de Maisonneuve, Amanda reached over and took Hart's hand. "You don't know, do you, Hart? Mummy died while you were away."

"Oh," he said. "When?"

"Just after Christmas. Neil was the last person to see her."

Hart glanced at Neil, who lowered his eyes. "She wasn't aware," Neil said. "She didn't speak directly to me."

"But you did get to meet her?" Hart asked.

"Oh yes."

"Did she *ever* speak to you?"

"Not really."

Amanda interjected, "Neil, I'm sure she knew you. Mother wrote Neil a letter, Hart. She instructed him to come here and get to know us all."

"I phoned her a few times from L.A.," Hart said, ruefully.

"Did she speak to you?"

"Not really. But I guess she recognised my voice."

"Oh dear," Amanda sighed. "A few days before she died, she came around again. She was her old self. I . . . I told her you were dead. So, she went to her grave thinking you were dead. She didn't mention you'd called."

Chez La Mère Michel was exactly as they're remembered, two small double rooms, softly lit and decorated with the cosy elegance of the best restaurant in a modest French provincial city, circa 1960s. The waiter showed them straight to their choice of table, number eight. No reservation necessary on a Saturday night? Hart thought it was a bad sign, but Amanda's eyes were shining, her belief in miracles reconfirmed by one more stroke of good fortune.

In the cab ride over, Neil had listened to the brother and sister arguing over the last scraps of their mother's attention. He wondered where the petulance came from. They'd had her all their lives. He'd known only a wizened old woman, and by then, she'd been unable to recognise him, or comprehend what he so desperately wanted to say. He carried a typewritten letter in his pocket bearing a wobbly signature, Kitty Granger – not exactly an invitation, it authorized him to contact her in Montreal. The wording was strangely formal, as though drafted by a lawyer. He didn't know – and now he never would – if his birth mother had been conscious of his existence, or whether kindly people looking after her had taken the decision to put his mind at ease.

From the moment he'd been told he was adopted, Neil had been making plans to find the woman he considered his "real" mother. Finding her became a quest. Amanda came closest to explaining his reasons when she spoke at Hart's memorial. Like the phantom brother Bill, his birth mother was, he felt sure, languishing somewhere. Waiting to be discovered. He was gripped by a sense of loss, of separation. He thought he could not be whole or calm until he found her.

By the time he summoned the courage to ask his adopted mother, Esther, for details, he was married with a baby of his own. Esther said little, except that his mother had been a teenager in trouble. From then on, Neil's obsession had fixed on the image of a desperate young girl. He knew the picture was false, she would be an old woman by now, but it was a girl's face he saw when he thought of her.

He'd gone to several expensive restaurants with Tom and Amanda and usually felt out of place, like a little boy with grownups. It wasn't an unpleasant sensation; he enjoyed their attention. But this was different. He studied the décor. The busy brocade wallpaper, ornate mouldings and gold-washed museum chairs looked exactly like an elegant, older woman's parlour. The room was small, a dozen tables and only half of them were occupied. The patrons were all in their sixties or older. For the first time since setting out on his quest, he was comfortable with what he'd found. Sitting at his mother's favourite restaurant table, he knew he was as close as he'd ever get to knowing who she was.

While Hart scrutinized the menu, Amanda talked nervously about things she thought might interest him, the NHL playoffs, Montreal's chances. The first of several futile attempts to pry him open, but he stayed blank, as if he was on the moon. Tom chatted with the waiter in French.

Neil sat still, trying to soak up every detail so he could reconstruct the room later in his mind's eye. He half regretted Wanda hadn't come along. He wished she'd been up to appreciating this experience, as a family. He had no idea what they were eating. Crème this, grillée à la whatever. It all tasted amazing. He savoured every bite, letting the others carry the conversation.

When the waiter brought a round of sumptuous pastries, the table fell quiet. Neil realised he hadn't been listening for some time. He drew himself up to his full height, which put him a good head above the others, and said, "I'm sure Mother sees us sitting here. She's watching us. She knows we're together." He faltered on the word mother, as though he'd never used it before.

Hart's lips spread into a tight smile. Tom and Amanda avoided each other's eyes. So Neil, who was sitting beside Amanda, reached down and took hold of her hand, lifted it up on to the table between them. His hand covered hers completely. Then he said, "Let us join together and thank the Lord for bringing us to this blessed moment."

Eager as always to salvage decorum, Tom grabbed Amanda's other hand, then Hart's. Both men squirmed. Hart lowered his eyes, and reached for Neil's with all the enthusiasm of a child who's sure the next few minutes are going to be painful.

Neil struck a sonorous tone. He knew they were all secretly laughing at him, and he did not give a damn.

"Thank you Lord, for bringing this family together at last. Please treat our mother well, as we know You will. Thank You for restoring brother Hart to us, whole and healthy. Have mercy on the departed soul amongst us. Amen."

The waiter watched from a discreet distance. As they tucked into their desserts, he came over to ask if anyone wanted a liqueur or coffee. Nods all around.

THIRTEEN

When Tom had settled the bill and they were out on the street again, Amanda suggested they go back to the hotel suite, but Hart said no, he'd made other arrangements.

"I don't want to be nosy," she said, unconvincingly. "But is that all the luggage you've got?" He was clutching the metal box of ashes, which Neil had rescued from the ballroom. Only then did he realise he must have left his suitcase and sleeping bag in the change room at Holt's.

"The rest of my stuff is back at my hotel," he muttered.

Amanda wanted desperately to prevent the reborn brother from wandering off into the night alone, but she couldn't think of anything more to say that didn't risk scaring him away for good. She invited him to meet them for breakfast in the hotel dining room. He nodded a half-hearted assent, shook Neil's hand, then Tom's.

Amanda hugged him and gushed, "I am so, so glad you're back." The hug was real enough but her voice was tentative, as though she didn't quite believe he was back, and maybe not for good. Tom led her away, towards Ste-Catherine Street. Neil followed. Hart strode off in the opposite direction, so that when Amanda turned back to look for him, all she saw was a little man burdened down with a heavy box.

"He knows where we are," said Tom, throwing his arm around her shoulders. "No more tears, okay? He's back to stay."

All things considered, Tom thought the evening had gone well. He was looking forward to hearing what Neil had to report from their hole-up in the men's room. At the corner, Amanda stopped. "Let's go back."

"Honey, don't smother him. He needs time."

"Did you give him any money?"

"He's not hungry. It's a lovely spring night, well above freezing. My guess is he'll be down in the hotel lobby when we get up. Hey, let's go to L'Express for a nightcap. Are you up for it, Neil?"

As the instant yes rolled off Neil's lips, Amanda reminded them that Wanda was still on her own, probably awake by now and starving.

When they got back to the hotel, she was gone. It was after midnight. Amanda insisted they go looking for her but Neil said, "It's no use. She's done this before, she'll be fine."

Her New York paranoia joining maternal concern, Amanda protested that a woman should not wander the streets alone after dark, and couldn't they both see she'd been upset? As Neil collapsed into an easy chair, Tom raided the mini-bar for a round of whiskies.

"I've had every booze under the sun," Neil sighed. "One more and I'm likely to throw – well, I won't sleep."

He took one anyway, telling himself it was only to be polite. He'd laboured through Sandrine's strange event, like a self-conscious adolescent out of his depth. The meal had woken him up. He knew there was still time for Wanda to ruin the night, but for the moment at least, he was just where he longed to be, alone with Amanda, and not too disappointed by Tom either, who'd done himself proud in the speech department.

Hardly had Neil settled in than it became clear the married enclave had expectations.

"So, tell us," Amanda started. "Where was Hart?"

"What do you mean?"

Tom was listening intently.

"Well, the two of you spent an awfully long time in the men's room. Come on, brother Neil, tell us what you know."

Neil tried not to squirm. "Not much, really. I think he said something about Vancouver."

"Vancouver!" Amanda winced. An east-coast type to the core, she could not picture Hart walking along the wrong ocean. Going outdoors in all seasons. Though he did look remarkably fit.

When she noticed Neil's attention drifting off to a semi-abstract rendering of mountains that hung above the TV set, she mustered her bossy-sister voice: "Neil! Tell us what Hart said. Where was he? Why did he come back now? Did he know Sandrine was planning a memorial?"

These mysteries had not troubled Neil.

"I'm kind of embarrassed to tell y'all this," he said, slipping into a drawl he'd picked up at bible camp, where confessions often made people weep. "We didn't actually get around to talking about where Hart was. I mean, a few things, yeah. Vancouver – guess I said that. He did get out to Vancouver. At least he was in – what'd he call it, Bee See? This time last week, he was there. He said the tulips are up."

He downed the whiskey. Tom moved quickly to pour another round.

"What did you talk about?" Amanda repeated, more slowly.

"Honey, that may not be any of our business," Tom interjected.

She ignored him, leaned ahead in her straight-backed chair, waiting for an answer.

"Well," Neil gulped. "Mainly we talked about me. I mean, I guess I did most of the talking. I told him a few things about what it was like growing up and not knowing where you're from. Who your people are. What kind of blood. Not that I'm prejudiced or anything, and I certainly had very, very great people to bring me up, which I guess is pretty obvious. Still, you always wonder. It's just that there's always something out there, you know, like a mist. Yeah, there's a mist around you all the time. You feel kind of, not at home. See, now that I know all of you, it's completely gone away. The mist. It's like I've always known you. And I would never have had that feeling otherwise. I'd have felt I missed something . . . . Hey, it just hit me. Mist like fog, sounds exactly like something you've missed . . ."

Amanda was stunned. That he had wanted to say these important things to a person of his own flesh and blood, she could easily believe. But that he'd chosen Hart? She could not picture Hart listening. This news was so unfair. The anger that had flown out of her in front of a hundred and fifty people now began to seep back.

"Were you two smoking pot in there?" she fired. "Is that what I smelled?"

Tom bit his lip. There were times when the open lines of marital communication tripped him up, and this was one of them.

"Pot?" Neil said, as if it were a curse. "Definitely not. It was something Hart got out on the coast. Medicinal, and totally legal. I forget what he said it was. Don't think you can get it up here."

Amanda looked at him incredulously. "Neil, let's start at the beginning, okay? Tell me everything Hart said to you. And you to him, of course. I'll make a nice pot of tea."

Tom hung his head. He knew exactly where this was leading, to a long night of tears and hugs, yet another epiphany for the epiphany-prone woman he had so gladly and successfully married. A wave of love would soon engulf them all. Before St. Neil could muster a shred of information about Hart's missing months, he stood up, yawned convincingly, and said good night.

What a good idea, he thought, to have taken a suite with a bed behind closed doors.

FOURTEEN

A minute after Hart had extricated himself from the dinner party and headed down the street, he wished he'd gone with them back to the hotel. The palliative effect of first class ganja had worn off during dinner. A headache was taking its place. He did not want to face the night alone, but when he looked back, they were heading cheerfully up Guy Street. Tom had his arm around Amanda, Neil bounced along beside her. Too late, he thought, and picked up the pace. A walk would do him good.

Though savoury to the palate, La Mère Michel's cuisine sat heavy in his stomach. Having scorned smoked meat, he had gone for the magret de canard, a reversal Tom and Amanda were quick to notice. He didn't care. He'd enjoyed that duck down to the bone.

Watching Neil royally stoned during a five-course French meal had been a delight. He was sure it explained the religious outburst preceding desert, though he'd felt it too, the ghostly presence of Kitty. As they ate, his brain kept playing old home movie footage, images of his mother in her prime, alive and vibrant. She had been a beautiful woman, by any standard. He had no trouble understanding how she'd slipped up on passion. But keeping the secret to herself had caused her such pain, and it leaked out onto everyone else. If only he'd known, he'd have put on a Neil Diamond record, twirled her around the kitchen and whispered in her ear, it doesn't matter.

Now she was gone, leaving them her secret, made flesh. Neil had suffered too, according to his voluminous confession in the men's room. There's something about toilets, he mused. The new desert, a place of exile fit for soul-searching. Sitting on the hard tile floor beside Neil, Hart had had flashes of déjà vu, which he did not attribute to weed. He had thought of René, the continuous flow of words that had attended his final weeks, while all he could do was sit and listen. Nature abhors a vacuum. If one man listens, the other will talk.

As he turned onto René Lévesque, he began to feel better. Striking out alone had been right after all, though the casket of ashes was heavier than it looked. Shifting the box to his other arm, he savoured a flashback. Night time in L.A., the dead man's final howl. Bodily functions speak louder than words, he chuckled to himself. Spewing an ungodly charge of banquet sweet-meats in front of everyone he'd ever known had been, he decided, a perfect tribute to a man who expired with a not dissimilar blast. Looked at one way, the memorial had offered a life-time guarantee: it was a scene of humiliation after which all other humiliations would pale.

At Dorchester Square, he veered off onto the lawn. He'd slept outside before. He knew how to stake out an obscure corner, root around for comfort and tune out street noise. But this was not the silly mock winter of Vancouver. Night reclaimed its kindred season. The snow had disappeared, but the ground was cold and uninviting. He decided to keep on walking.

At St-Laurent Boulevard. there was no longer much danger of running into anyone he knew. As he headed up to the intersection of Ste-Catherine and the Main, the scenery suddenly improved. After midnight, the clubs were letting out. He turned east, onto a dense block of sex shops and porn cinemas, strip clubs and karaoke bars. The streets were packed with slick-haired birds weighed down with tattoos and chains. More gangs than couples. Some were women, others wished they were. He swam in the crowd like a man who belonged, keeping his chin up, gazing at oddities from the corner of his eye.

A towering red-head with massive shoulders stood beside a half-open door. Fish net stockings on Doric column legs appeared a few inches below her crotch and ended in size eleven stilettos. Flashing a coy smile, she invited him to come upstairs, in French.

"Rien dans les culottes!" he answered with an apologetic shrug, gripping an empty handful of denim in his crotch.

She laughed. "Pauvre 'tit garcon. I've got enough for the two of us."

Walking on by, he thought of Tom's eulogy – their so-called tour of Village transvestite bars. Not quite the way he remembered the evening. In Hart's recollection, Tom had been tense; they were both tense. A big-ticket New York attorney out on the town with his new wife's brother, how could they relax? The so-called girls weren't the point. The real issue had been Amanda. Despite their big society wedding, Hart still had trouble picturing his little sister belonging to another man. Why even try to picture it? She'd disappeared, that's all. Those two were tight as a knot, spoke to each other in glances, most unsubtle, as if the rest of the world were blind.

Then he saw her, no more than twenty feet ahead, teetering, glowering, as hungry and lethal as any other denizen of the night. Neil's long-lost, possibly demented wife. What was her name?

"Hiya! Jeeze! Imagine meeting you here!" She leaned into him and cackled.

Wanda was shorter than Hart, and just as thin. Her hair was thin too, long around the sides but short and flyaway on top, copper blonde, electrified. She was wearing a purple coat, fitted at the waist and buttoned tight, a voluble gypsy skirt peeking out around the hem. Her teeth were chattering. The most striking part of her appearance was her large green eyes, wild, and echoed by a pair of clam-shaped earrings. On closer inspection, Hart saw that they were in fact two halves of the same clam, hooked through holes in her ears.

"You don't even know who I am," she wagered. She was chewing gum.

"Sure," he said. "How could I forget?"

She giggled. "How *could* you forget? I was the one who spotted you first. Did you hear me scream?"

"Was that you?" he said, as if it had been a great achievement. "Well, I definitely heard the scream."

"I've never seen anybody puke like that. I mean, so much of it! What did you do, clean out the whole buffet? Look, I got a shrimp stain on my skirt."

"I'm sorry," he said.

"Go on, it was worth it. Say. Did you plan to show up like that?"

"Not exactly."

"No kidding! They all thought you were dead."

"Did they." His voice flattened out at the reminder of inquisitions to come.

"You planned the whole thing, didn't you?"

Few varieties of instinct were available to Hart, but he was a natural improviser. He'd always known he would fail miserably at crime, which is harder than it looks and requires a great deal of planning. Spontaneous combustion was his forte. He felt the prick of invention as keenly as a pregnant woman feels her first contraction, and was similarly unable to stop what came next.

As she stood there, hugging her coat in the heart of red-light Montreal, it dawned on Hart that this woman knew almost nothing about him. He could say whatever came to mind, decide whether it sounded plausible, try it out on her. And if it sounded wrong, or he changed his mind in the morning, whose version would be believed?

Suddenly he remembered her name. "Wanda!" he cried. "Why don't we get a coffee?"

She was startled. "Where do you want to go?"

"How about right here?" They were standing in front of a coffee shop, La Belle Province, brightly lit and brimming with animated nighthawks.

"Wait a minute." He paused on the threshold. "I lost my wallet."

"Don't worry about it." She took him by the arm, wheeled him inside. "I've got lots of money. As a matter of fact, I've got lots of *your* money." Then she laughed, a shriek that turned heads.

"How's that?" He was compelled to ask.

Waving a bank card, she grinned. "Amanda split her share of the legacy with (she spat out his name) Neil. My ex-husband."

Hart's shock registered as incomprehension. So Wanda continued. "You know, your will? Since you were 'dead' (she made little quotes in the air with her fingers) they read your will and gave out all your stuff, money, stocks, et cetera, as per orders. Seems you were doing pretty well at the time of your 'death.'"

Then she laughed again, this time covering her mouth with her hand, as though the news was embarrassing. Hart wasn't sure whether she was laughing at him, or at some vast cosmic joke in which he played a minor role. They took their coffee and a sugary doughnut to a table at the back of the room.

Minutes after sitting down, Hart knew his fantasies of spinning simple Wanda a spur-of-the moment account of his travails on the West Coast was just that, a fantasy. There were several reasons why Wanda Bell Springer was unable to absorb his account of the past, some going back as far as her childhood, which she would gladly do, if Hart was prepared to listen. She came from a long line of suffering women for whom men were plentiful, unchangeable, and ultimately, dispensable. She did not suffer from the urban educated woman's liability of having too many choices, therefore she had never needed to learn the simple secret of pleasing a man: let him talk about himself. Encourage him with intelligent questions, smile and sigh, but listen. Instead, Wanda relied on the high-school logic that if a guy agreed to drink a coffee with you, then he wanted something. And he could damn well take what was on offer.

Even so, in the case of Hart Granger, she genuinely wondered about his mysterious absence, his sudden, unexpected re-appearance. Had he wanted to talk, she might have let him. But Wanda's mind was elsewhere.

Two hours before stumbling upon Hart, she had woken up in the empty hotel suite and discovered the others had come and gone. Poking around the high-priced furnishings, she wandered into Amanda and Tom's room, found their genuine leather travel bags gaping open in reproof. She tried out Amanda's perfume. She helped herself to the rouge. On the back of the door she found a notice revealing how hideously expensive the suite was, and vowed to act on these insults. Distance herself from pretentious people who had nothing to do with her. They weren't her people, and in a way, neither was Neil. The insight came as a sudden, powerful revelation, possibly from the Lord. She had not stopped to enquire. She had known for a while what she had to do. Now she saw the moment had come. Even if it meant losing contact with her children for a time, she was sure they would come around.

Wanda carried her decision from the Delta hotel on Avenue President Kennedy (a very significant address, she later remarked), to rue Bleury, a name she found equally if not more significant. Then onto Ste-Catherine, the patron saint of children, or so she'd learned at bible school from a girl whose parents had been Catholic. By the time she met Hart, she'd spent an hour stumbling around the hallucinogenic hub of a foreign city. Fluorescent lights of revelation burned brightly in her soul. Startled by his sudden appearance, she soon saw that this, too, was meant to be.

She sank her index finger into the frosty doughnut, and raised it to her lips. "I'm sure you heard me say back there, 'my ex-husband?'"

Everything Wanda said seemed to require quotation marks. Hart wondered if he should reply in italics.

"I *did*, he said. "I *noticed*. When did this happen?"

"I guess it happened to me while you guys were eating at that fancy restaurant. Oh, yeah, I knew. I found the note:

'Jump in a cab. We're out on the town.' 'We' – the whole fucking family, I presume."

"I was there," he admitted, regretting it immediately. This would not only imply interest in the conflict, it would implicate him in the raw proceedings.

"Fucking, fucking family."

"Wanda!"

"I'm sorry. Are you religious?"

"No."

"Me neither. Not really. Neil is, so I went along with it. You know what the last thing the Lord said to me? He said, Wanda, kick that son-of-a-bitch out of your life. Over and out. God."

She laughed, an extended eruption of hiccup chortles. This time, Hart laughed too, hoping that by sharing a joke, he might be able to change the subject. While she wiped her eyes he racked his brain for an alternative subject, finding none. Then he noticed she wasn't wiping away tears of laughter, she was crying. He handed her a table napkin. She blew her nose loudly. Two deep streaks of mascara had travelled down her cheeks to her chin.

"Your eye makeup's running," he said.

She took the crumpled napkin and smeared mascara around her face. Then she rubbed her eyes, creating big racoon circles of charcoal. He gave up, focused his gaze on the coffee mug.

"I need a refill," she said, snapping her fingers at the kid behind the counter. When their cups were steaming again, Wanda picked up the story she'd started telling her friend Marie, who had more or less written her off. First she filled Hart in on the sunny side of love with Neil, just enough detail to set the scene. Then she launched into a description of his behaviour, beginning with the day he hired a detective to track down his birth mother. There had been a letter. Yes, the woman had written back to Neil, saying she'd be glad to meet him. He did, and moved his attention elsewhere.

As Wanda talked, Hart got a complete picture of the other side of the mirror. Whereas most metaphors fade under careful consideration, this one held up. He saw his own face reflected in Wanda's anguish. Her hostility equalled his. Irrational, therefore all the more powerful. He was on the other side now, staring at an opaque silver wall. By the time Wanda started to wind down, exhausted by her own account, he knew more or less what he had to say.

He reached over and took hold of her hand. She froze. "Wanda," he said. "Under no circumstances can you leave Neil."

He squeezed. It hurt, but she didn't dare budge.

"Why not?" The words were dry.

Hart let a few seconds pass, stared into her eyes until she was forced to look away.

"Because," he said, as if that were reason enough. Then he let go of her hand. She was still wearing her wedding rings, and reached down to straighten the diamond which, since she'd lost so much weight, tended to slip around.

"You are *not* going to leave Neil," he continued, authoritatively. "I don't want to hear any more bullshit about what the *Lord* did or did not *say*. This is your brother-in-*law* speaking. No leaving Neil . . . You know why, don't you?"

She nodded, but looked mystified.

"Because there is just too, too much love between the two of you."

He let the revelation hang in the air, like a dripping carcass dangling on a meat hook. Wanda's eyes widened.

"Leave Neil, and you'll never get over it. Neither will he."

Her lips went slack, eyebrows shot up.

"You think so?" she said, meekly.

"Look at me," he said. A rhetorical command, her eyes bored through him like a starvation photo.

"I am a victim of divorce. You saw where that leads. My jaw still aches."

She laughed. Bad sign, he thought. Humour will lighten the moment and this conversation could go on all night.

He scowled. "Neil and I had a long talk after the ah, speeches, et cetera. He told me a few things about you two, what you mean to him. He dearly wishes you would resume your wifely duties and forget all about whatever you've been going through."

He grinned slightly, to clarify what he meant by 'wifely duties.' She brightened.

"He said that?"

"In the way guys say that sort of thing, yes, he did. Neil is a *man*, Wanda."

He took a sip of tepid coffee, letting the news sink in.

"Look, I know you can't stand Amanda. She has that effect on some people. It's a secondary effect. Most people like her. You will too, once you get to know a few things about her, things she doesn't tell people unless you really get to know her."

Wanda's eyebrows shot up. "Such as?"

"It's not my place to reveal Amanda's private woes, but I am sure that in due time she will confide in you. You won't be able to stop her."

"She hates me."

"She does not."

"She laughs at me, and at Neil. So do you."

"You give yourself too much credit, Wanda. I'm far too obsessed with my own shaky problems. I'm hardly in a position to laugh at anybody. I'm dead, for chrissakes"

She laughed. "You are far from dead, mister."

"Dead meat, I think they say. Washed up. Not to mention broke. See, there I go, obsessing about myself. My point is, Neil. Neil is sending a message via me, a message of love and reconciliation to his cherished wife. And I talk about my problems."

Hart reached out for the bill, which had been revised three times.

"Face facts, Wanda," he said, edging out of the booth. "Like it or not, you're family. We're family. Always will be, no matter where you run. If you leave Neil now, your kids will stay in touch and they will bring you news, and that's all you'll have to go on. Snippets. Okay, your choice. Just don't imagine you can get away from any of us."

He spoke in the tone of a doomed man, a man who knows he is lecturing himself.

For Wanda it was better than a bear hug. He nodded sagely, picked up the box of ashes, and slid out of the booth.

At the counter, he realised he had no money. He went back to the table, and set the bill down in front of Wanda.

"You'll have to take care of this."

"Oh, yeah, sure," she replied sheepishly, as if St. Francis of Assisi had had to ask for help.

"We're expected for breakfast at the hotel," he said. "Will I see you there?"

"You will," she promised, in a whisper heavy with repentance.

As he walked out into the glow of Ste-Catherine Street, he noticed his shoes were sticking to the pavement. Continuing toward the Main, he tried to remember where he'd met the red-haired beauty with balls. She/he too might need to talk. When he came to where they'd met, the door was closed. There were lights on upstairs.

Raising the load to his shoulder, he turned and headed toward Mount Royal. In an hour or so, daylight would poke through. The box was light, the field wide open.

EPILOGUE

Eighteen Rosa-Luxenbergstrasse.

The German girl's address comes back to Hart as he is tucking into a business-class breakfast on an overnight flight to Frankfurt. A headline in a German-language newspaper catches his eye, and calls up the detail. He scribbles the address on a napkin, sure it will slip away as easily as it came to him.

That strange encounter in Venice, California. Three years later, it seems like an old movie.

In the months that followed his return, he paid the price of dying. He refused to touch a penny of his former money, though the beneficiaries offered to give it back. He went to work for Vince and in due time, bought him out and turned the office back to its former rugged glamour. René's paintings enjoy prominent exposure in the new décor. His brother's ashes have been scattered on his grave.

Hart's reborn company is called OANN, an acronym of *Okanch amamoweech nda ndouie,* the dead musician's name. It's Cree for Animals Gathering Together in the Wilds, an inside joke Hart savours every time he is called upon to explain the meaning to a group of business types. Since OANN Inc. specializes in investing capital raised from the development of natural resource energy, Hart travels often to James Bay, Great Whale, points north. He sits on committees and heads up syndicates. He has made a horde of full-blooded Cree investors very rich. If all goes as planned, he'll soon bring Europe into the loop. Germany first. The Germans are thrilled to be doing business with First Nation peoples.

Leni? Lena Aurbach. That was her name. As the plane touches ground, Hart remembers.

He wonders how she is, whether she knows he is alive, and if not, has the grim spectacle of a man's death darkened her life? He re-plays the scene from beginning to end, a full-colour memory of dazzling sun on water, radiant white-hot hair. Her smooth, lanky legs as she reached down to give her steak to the dog. How she looked at the dog, petted its mane, then back in his direction, all of it reflected in the plate glass door.

Suddenly it dawns on him: she was watching, she met his gaze, reflected in the mirror of the door. She wasn't blind. Of course not! A blind girl, travelling alone with a dog? How could he ever have believed . . . ?

As the plane pulls to a stop, relief floods over him, as though he'd come upon a true story that ended happily. Then it hits him: if she wasn't blind, *that means I was blind*. Mock affliction, transferred from a fanciful girl to the man she had chosen to dupe. The irony gives him great satisfaction.

Matters of Heart

ACKNOWLEDGEMENTS

Many people have read and commented upon various drafts of this novel or contributed in other significant ways. I would like to thank them all, including John Aylen, Felicity Fanjoy, Tomson Highway, Maureen Rump, Cathy Knight, Kent Stetson, Lesley McCubbin, Rana Bose, Pasha Malla, Sheila Moore, Sam Sala, Lawrence Paul Yuxweluptun, Rhiannon Gwyn, Michaela Cornell, Janet Harron, Michael Callaghan, and especially my publisher and editor, Kim McArthur. I am grateful to The Canada Council for support. A warm thank you to Gwyn Campbell, who gallantly accepted the presence of another man in our life during the creation of *Matters of Hart*.

Marianne Ackerman